GUARDIAN OF THE PLANETOIDS

Book 1: Spirit Forest

Jhonny Steppes

PLANETOID: SPIRIT FOREST Copyright © 2024 by Alexander J. McCarty

ISBN 978-1-943733-49-1

Published by Sphere of Compassion, Inc.
https://sphereofcompassion.com
authoralexandermccarty@gmail.com
https://facebook.com/authoralexandermccarty
http://www.instagram.com/gabriel_of_the_exps
http://www.instagram.com/sphere_of_compassion
https://twitter.com/of_the_Exps
linktr.ee/SphereofCompassion/

Cover Artist
Innovator 123
https://x.com/armandosionosa?lang=en

Books from *Sphere of Compassion*

THE MAIN CHARACTER!

Hero's Epic Journey Arc

1. *The Hero's Epic Journey Begins*:
2. *The Hero's Epic Journey Continues*:

The Main Character: Legendary Origin Stories!

-1. *Guardian Angel:*

-2. *Broad Spectrum Assassin*:

The Main Character Manga

1. The Main Character The Manga Issue 1
2. The Main Character The Manga Issue 2
3. The Main Character The Manga Issue 3
4. The Main Character The Manga Issue 4
5. The Main Character The Manga Vol1 (ISSUE 1-6)

OF THE EXPS

Rebellion Arc

1. *Exp 8*: **Rebellion of the Exps**

Resurrection Arc

2. *The Hero of Sel*: **Resurrection of the Exps**
3. *Sellum*
4. *Destruction, Creation, Absence*

Origins of The Exps

1. *Fate's Apotheosis: Origins of the Exps*

Rise Arc

5. *Sacrificial Savior*

Manga of the Exps

1. *Awakening* (Fall 2023)
2. *The Crimson Coliseum*

Table of Contents

EXTRAS

Introduction

I first read this novel in 2019 soon after making friends with the writer. I wanted so badly to have a physical version to enjoy and share with the world. Thankfully, after purchasing the rights, that dream is now a reality! We are very happy to bring this story to new life! The writer also wrote _On The Plus Side Series_!

We really hope you enjoy!

"Special thanks to Michael and Alex for helping me edit this book and giving me suggestions on how to make it better. To my best friend, Frank, for putting up with all my previous attempts at writing (and being the best supporter I could ask for,) and Miyazaki and Aaron Ehasz for inspiring me to write this story in the first place."

This book is dedicated to those who are burdened with great responsibility. May you find those who support you and make that burden lighter. Be proud of what you've accomplished and don't let worries of the future impede your path.

DEATH OF A PLANETOID

Chapter 0

A long-eared rag doll glided along the ocean in a small wooden boat. It wasn't the current that was guiding it along its path. A young elven child, who stood at the shoreline, was willing it to move with her magic. She had short, brown hair and big, blue eyes and a thirst for adventure. A solitary fish tattoo partially disguised by her shirt's neckline shimmered and swayed with the movement of her hands.

An elven man with long and greying hair lounged in the sun and watched with one eye as the young girl carried on with childlike frustration.

"The boat, I can't get it to come back," she cried.

The elder rose from the light pink island palm and straightened his spine. He was half listening and half enjoying the tropical winds that were cooling him on that warm day.

"Think about your tattoo. You're a small minnow in a vast open sea. Your movement, little one, depends more on the ebb and flow of the ocean itself."

The child stood silently; her light blue eyes were aglow. She was a good-hearted child who at this point in her life listened when someone taught her something.

"A small creature learns to ride the tide, not fight it," the elder continued. "That is how our small planet exists in the grand scheme of things. Our planet fitting into its place leads to greater harmony in the Big Dream."

This metaphor weighted too heavily on the child's mind. She frowned. "Can you just tell me how to move the boat already? I had it working, but then it just quit on me."

"Precocious just like your parents," the elder chortled. "They wanted to investigate the Ocean's Gate today. I don't know why."

He looked out onto his village. It was a tightly connected network of colorful seashell homes with wooden bridges that ran across the sea and connected to their little island. Some plank pathways were fractured and lead nowhere.

"The danger is but a memory. Our priority should be to rebuild. We must focus on the future rather than the past," the elder remarked to himself.

As if by cruel irony, his body and voice were shaken by an underground tremor. The surface of the water wavered and rippled and the young girl's boat overturned and her doll floated up facedown. The young girl cried as it happened. The ground shook so hard, her little body fell down; and cautiously, the old man leapt to his feet.

He listened closely with his long and veiny ears as he heard a series of explosions, each setting another off in a series of chain reactions mightier and more fearsome than the last. Then everything went silent.

The teacher and his apprentice stood silently, fearing even the smallest movement could become a ripple that'd evoke the planet's instability further.

"I want you to come to me," the elder said softly, pulling his fingers forward.

The little girl was filled with the kind of terror that children experience when they cannot comprehend their surroundings. Tears began to well up in her eyes and she whimpered quietly. "I want my mommy. I want daddy. Where are they?"

The old man swallowed, forcing a stoic expression.

A mighty crack appeared and sliced through the pink tree's roots. The tree split apart, and the elder grabbed the girl up in his hands.

The crack traveled into the water; and suddenly, the fault line descended with water rushing downward like a waterfall, taking the boat and doll with it.

"Dollia!" She reached out, trying to will it back to her with the magic she learned.

The elder kept running, dashing along from the fractured island onto the shifting wooden planks. The young girl thrashed and struggled in his arms, flailing in a tantrum of misery.

He held her comfortingly with arms quaking with worry.

He rushed through the village, taking every shortcut he knew. There were women and children running frantically and chanting for protection.

"Jeeg!" A middle aged, plump elven woman cried out to him. "What is happening to our world?"

Jeeg swallowed hard, panic filling his eyes. "This might have to do with the Ocean's Gate."

"Didn't the Tintels go down to investigate it a few hours ago?"

"Where's mommy?! Where's daddy?!" The young Tintel sobbed and pounded the air.

The middle-aged woman's body trembled and her voice shook. "What are we going to do?!"

Jeeg put his hand upon her shoulder. "If the plates of Tarabos are sinking, try to get to higher ground on your gliders. The Sylphens have blessed them with their magic. We are in this together."

The middle-aged woman nodded and dashed off in the direction of her sea shell house. Jeeg ran in the opposite direction, heading to the Tintel's abode.

He had a made a promise to Krithaan Tintel, the patriarch of the family. He could still hear the words of Krithaan in his head: "If we don't make it back, protect my daughter at all costs."

Jeeg rushed into the wooden door of a tall, teal and spiraling sea shell home. Inside, in the midst of a well-kept house was a small triangular mini-ship with a pilot and passenger bubble at the center. He had flown in it once with Aerie Tintel, a young mother fascinated by technology from other planets.

Jeeg quickly opened the hatch and placed the crying child in the passenger seat. He moved into the bubble himself and pressed the center button on the control board.

Light focused on the front barrel and then emitted out as a laser that blasted the front of the house open.

The young child desperately hid her face in silence.

Jeeg pulled the levitation switch on the mini-ship and it began to glide. It dragged for a bit on the ground before lifting into the air and flying through the burned and ruined entrance of the little girl's house

Jeeg took off into the purpling sky, full of dark unsettling clouds that stretched into demonic faces. He looked down to see plates of the planet now lowering into the dark abyss below them.

Frantic flyers buzzed around like helpless insects. His shoulders dropped and he bowed his head in lament. He held deep regret for being a survivor. He had escaped when there were thousands more deserving to leave this imploding world. All the while, the young child bawled, her voice growing quite hoarse, not realizing that no matter how loud she screamed it would not bring her parents back.

Jeeg took one final glance at his world...now fractured into continents just as once was ideologically.

"All those years of building bridges...only for nature to...destroy everything."

He saw the Acridian desert, a home to many adventures he had in his youth. He and a boy he was fond of braved the dry wilderness of sand sharks in order to find the lost Jewel of Acridia hidden deep within a buried stone temple. The sand of the desert was now sliding into an abyss like a freshly gaping sinkhole the size of half the planet.

Jeeg looked and saw the once great levitating city of Argon, made of dark rectangular towers lit by magical gases. He recalled how in his youth he s firsthand how these gasses were made and modified to kept the city afloat. It too could not resist the gravitational pull of the ether and crashed into the Oceanita, causing a massive wave of white foam.

Many sea shell homes including Jeeg's hometown were swept away in the enormous tidal wave.

Jeeg cried into his hands with unbound grief. This watery world, the great Oceanita, was home to the people and the places he cherished most, both living and dead.

From the stratosphere, a once fruitful and prosperous planet split apart and imploded on itself, taking an innumerable number of lives with it. The tiny minnow no longer coexisted in the big sea. It had been torn apart without cruel pre-meditation.

He watched the world's remnants disperse.

This universe of planetoids was just as unpredictable and fleeting.

Life was, as a whole, uncontrollable.

THE VILLAGE EMISSARY

Chapter 1

A planetoid of lush green and the purest blue slowly twirled in the dark vastness of space. Fresh water rushed through the rivers, filling the lakes. The ground brimmed with trees as white and smooth as porcelain. Their palm leaves were a rainbow of colors. From them hung fruits in the shape of blue and white tear drops. The boars of the forest were head-butting the trees to dislodge the glowing fruit. Above the treetops Wyrmwolves were circling. These purple winged canines with dragon-like snouts divebombed, snatching a juicy fruit in mid-flight. lived off the mysterious fruit.

The cycle of life was never interrupted or broken. With the advent of a small village of humanoids, a compromised existence with nature was formed.

From wooden cabins by the lakeside, the villagers emerged every morning. The Men wore silky tunics and patchwork pants. The women were clad in dresses of simple patterns, stitched by the village seamstresses. They were eager to begin their harvest of soul fruits and their caretaking of the fertile spirit trees that came with it, but none were more eager than Aya Tintel.

Greeting the villagers, the young woman stood apart from them. She was considerably taller with tanned skin intertwined with numerous inked tattoos poking out of the exposed parts of her body. The fish tattoos were shaped like a diamond with an incomplete triangle for a tail

8

fin. They were drawn in a way to appear as if they were swimming across her muscular mid-riff.

Her large round eyes, as blue as an ocean in the sun, brimmed with a deep empathy. Her brown hair was cut in a multicolored bob with the tips dyed the hue of the berries she loved most in the forest. Sticking out of her hair were two long pointy ears. In her hand, she clutched a staff cut from a spirit tree. Its wispy white wood possessed a commanding presence that gave her confidence simply by clenching it.

"What's the consensus for the harvest?" she inquired to an unshaven forty-year-old man wearing a hat woven from golden straw. "Do you think we'll have covered all the trees with star dust and picked before the season ends?"

The man laughed. "Lookit you, Aya. I'm surprised how invested you are in our work, considerin' all ya do is guard us from those beasties."

Aya gave a warm smile that betrayed her warrior garb. "Allons, you know how much I love this planetoid and everyone on it. We're all brothers and sisters in the big dream."

The man twirled a stem of a soul fruit between his teeth with his tongue, and spoke with a drawn-out accent. "Relax, Aya. You always make sure I take an extra helping of stardust with me when we go out to the forests. If anything, they'll be over-dusted."

"Better over dusted than withering over the wintertime and not coming back," Aya said, clutching her staff. "But you already knew that."

"I did. I knew it the first two hundred times ya said it," Allons snapped, before he was interrupted.

"Aieeeee! Get this monster away from me!"

9

Aya leapt to attention, with her staff held defensively, and her bare feet firm on the ground. "Well, duty calls. Don't be late," she said, her hand in the air, signaling an affirmative before dashing off.

"That girl is so spirited. I think she gets tipsy on the juice from them trees. I'd probably be just as hopped up if I was on her diet," muttered Allons

Allons' middle-aged wife stood next to him and growled. "It's better than all the alcohol you suck down."

Aya dashed across the dirt road, kicking up dust before stopping where she heard a feminine shriek.

Standing and shaking was a young woman like Aya. Not only did her pale skin and naturally ginger hair differ from her elven friend, the clothes she wore were reserved and refined. She sported a light green sundress with a matching floppy hat filled with bright spring flowers. Her hazel eyes were even wider than Aya's, and not just because of how terrified she was.

"My stars, Aya," she cried in a high voice that was heightened further in fear. "Please, get this horrifying monster away from me."

Aya slid to the left of this young woman to see the threat behind the woman's flowery sundress. It was a small canine creature with pink fur lined from its muzzle to its short stubby tail. It growled and yipped at the woman in the sandals, hovering with little wings in order to nip at her.

Aya narrowed her eyes. She pursed her lips in disproval. "Really Flora? A Wyrmwolf pup? This furry friend hasn't even turned purple yet."

"Ayaaa," the woman whined and shuffled her feet in flighty fashion. "You know how I feel about those monsters."

She lowered her left hand, the hand she held at her breast and pulled her white glove forward to show a thick bite mark.

Aya's eyes were diluted with compassion. "I wasn't there when that Wyrmwolf attacked you, but I won't let you get hurt again." She held Flora tenderly to her bosom. "I swear upon my honor as an Aquan."

Flora hugged Aya firmly and looked up at her. "You'll have to be my personal protector then."

Aya tapped Flora's nose. "Or you'll have to stay out of trouble."

The towering elven woman walked over to the baby pup.

The pup was still trying his hardest to get Flora's attention by chewing on her dress.

Aya took her staff and pounded the ground, causing the air to become brisk and pillowy. A breeze blew through the center of all three lifeforms and the tension between the Wyrmwolf and Flora dissolved.

The creature, having been calmed, flew off on its stubby fairy-like wings.

Flora began to hold down her dress which billowed as the breeze blew. She then sighed. "I love when you do that, Aya. My stress just blows away when you stamp that shiny staff." Her hazel eyes grew half lidded with relaxation. "How in the world does it do that again?"

Aya smiled from ear to ear. "We're all interconnected in this universe, Flor. We all have souls at our center. This staff, made from the wood of an Atma tree, contains properties that soothe the soul."

"No matter how many times I hear it, still casts a spell on me. I really need to get me one of my own," Flora gushed. "Sorry. I even get the vapors when I thread clothing wrong. I'm just a very giddy person."

Aya smiled and patted Flora's exposed back. "I'll be happy to use it anytime you want, Flor."

The young woman smiled and her eyes sparkled as they looked at her friend. The two had known each other for years, but every day they were still learning stuff about each other.

"You're the best. I shoulda just asked before. I was just so nervous that you'd say no," said Flora, looking down with flushed cheeks.

"Well, hey, now you know. However, I can't let you use it. It's a part of me, Flora," Aya said, waving her finger.

Flora smiled, grabbing the staff. "Not even a touch?"

Aya heard the cries of a child playing and began walking towards the lakeside. "Would you do me a favor."

"Sure. What?"

Aya spoke with her back turned. "Please don't scream like that again over tiny animals. You made me think that a Noctursa had finally broken its sleep schedule."

"O-oh-kay," Flora said, shuffling in her shoes to catch up to her friend. "I promise."

The two reached the lakeside where they observed gorgeous water sparking in the distance. Small islands with a few trees floated slowly in the distance. Hearing a little peep, Aya and Flora looked down and saw a young boy. He had scruffy orange hair and a dark blue bathing suit patterned with floral designs similar to the fruit growing on the spirit trees.

"Hey ladies," said the boy with a toothy grin. "What brings you to my resort?" His feet stood on the stone filled sand as water rushed over them.

Flora held her hands to her chest and whined with frantic anxiety. "Jaz, don't play out here. I was face to face with a monster a few minutes earlier."

Aya rolled her big blue eyes and stepped into the water, feeling it with her own bare feet. "Jaz here is just enjoying the cool water on his toes. He appreciates nature's bath water."

"Of course I am!" yelled Jaz and he jumped in place, making a big splash, causing water droplets to land on Aya and Flora. The latter gave an eek. "I'm also planning how I can claim Jaz Island."

"Jaz Island!?" Both women asked with an arched eyebrow.

"The third island floating over there. I'm going to claim it," Jaz said, pointing excitedly to the third flying island. "And I'll swing on that big palm tree."

Flora's eyes grew wide and frantic. "No, you're not! Why can't you just play in the village with your brothers and sisters?"

Aya smiled and lifted her staff. "Relax Flora, he has no way of getting there." A wily glint appeared in Aya's eyes. "Unless he gets some help from someone incredible."

"Oh no, no no no," Flora said, shaking her head again. "Please don't do it."

Aya positioned her staff over the water like she was about to part it.

Jaz and Flora both gasped as they saw Aya's fish tattoos move their fins.

"I love this part!" Jaz loudly exclaimed.

"I don't," Flora quietly murmured as a large bubble raised out of the water.

Aya deftly guided it with her staff and moved it closer to Jaz.

Flora shielded her eyes as Aya smiled and told Jaz to "Hop in."

The boy dived into the bubble and Aya moved it down so he could poke his head out and breath. His little gap tooth was proudly on display with a big grin on his face.

Aya looked down and grinned. "Now are you ready to fly to the Island?"

The boy nodded with great excitement. He closed his eyes as Aya counted down, "Okay, one, two, three." The bubble moved forward a tiny bit before dispersing back into the lake, leaving Jaz standing in shallow water. With his eyes still closed, he asked. "Am I there yet?"

"Open your eyes," Aya responded.

Jaz surveyed the land and water he was in. "What happened?" He asked with innocent disappointment.

"I got too tired to zoom you all the way to the island," said Aya in a mock-exasperated voice while resting her staff and her hands on her tattooed knees. "Bubble magic takes a lot out of you."

"Liar, I've seen you travel in bubbles before," the boy whined in an octave similar to Flora's.

Aya sighed. "I can't just let you travel on your own. I think your sister would pop a blood vessel."

"I think I already have," Flora responded with her hand to her head, half-jokingly.

Aya placed her hand on the dejected Jaz's shoulder. "Look, I promise we'll travel to the island one day, but you have to do me a favor."

The boy's eyes widened with excitement, "What is it? Oh, please tell me?"

"You'll have to play in the village with the rest of your family," Aya said and Flora smiled in approval.

"You're so cool, Aya. I'd totally invite you to my island," The boy said and he flashed his nonexistent muscles and ran off towards the wooden cabins.

"How sweet, but remember Jaz, that island isn't yours!" Aya hollered after him. "We share that land with everyone on this planetoid."

Flora giggled. "Well, Aya. Looks like you have an admirer, and some competition when it comes to muscles." She eyed Aya's thighs.

Aya scoffed in return, laying her hands behind her head and relaxing her eyes while her staff magically floated in place. "As if. I'll be forced to retire when a man in this village can take me on." She opened her eyes casting them towards the village. "Well, other than my teacher."

"Speaking of Jeeg," Flora said in deep thought. "I haven't seen him all morning."

Aya tossed her hands up and aside. "I'm sure he's trying to get out of his work. Lazy old man. The ancients know I'm not going to be able to soothe all these beasts on my own."

Aya dashed back in the direction of town, with Flora trailing after her while holding her dress flaps. "Come on, Aya. You know, I can't run in this dress!"

"Don't wear one then," Aya shot back with a playful flick of her tongue.

"Some of us like being ladies, Aya." Flora sighed and picked up her shoes. She ran with them in hand to try and keep up.

"There are all kinds of ladies in this world, Miss prim and proper." Aya turned around and without warning, she scooped up Flora in her arms with a simple sweep off her feet. "Some are just cooler than others."

Flora gasped and hollered. "Aya, what are you doing?!"

"The coolest ones are also the most responsible. We have to carry the burdens of others," Aya said with a mischievous grin as her friend frantically tapped on her arm to let her go.

"Aya, come on. You know I'm going to get sick, Ayaaaa!"

Aya didn't listen, but dashed even faster, heading towards the heart of the small village.

She slowed down and scoured the buildings. All were made of the same spirit wood as her staff. Aya begrudgingly accepted that they had been cut down for the villagers. A single staff of spirit wood was one thing. She had gone through a ceremony that her mentor had instructed her to do in order to gain the tree's acceptance of its fate. Those cabins had been there before she and Jeeg had arrived.

She walked to the center of the town where she found Jeeg sitting at a stone garden by the town's fruit's hoister. With close cropped silver hair cut that reflected his age, large pointed ears and a small metallic band around his head, he resembled an old wise sage. He looked striking in his shining purple robe. It contrasted with his ridged tan skin that wrinkled up like a tree in its elder years.

He relayed a story to the new students of the colony in a way that made Aya's own ears stand-up.

"I grasped young Aya's hand as the waters around us grew highly unstable. I knew something disastrous was happening. They raged like a tempest. Something deep below the waters had been disturbed and as I surveyed the planet, I knew nature's balance had become unhinged. Our sea shell homes collapsed from violent earthquakes under the water, and there were just seconds before I reached an emergency escape ship. As we left the planet, I watched as the planet implode from the core, leaving nothing but fractured islands of crumbling land. The story is bittersweet, however. As we searched the black sky, we were fortunate to come across this beautiful land and before long, we had gained acceptance from your families. This has been our new home for the last fifteen years."

Aya's face wretched as she heard these words from the old storyteller. She dropped her friend on the ground who gasped loudly.

"Oh, sweet stable ground!" Flora raised her voice.

Aya looked briskly at the old man. "Jeeg, why don't you tell them a better story? Like one for calculating the sequence of seeds within a soul fruit?"

Jeeg gave a deep, raspy but friendly laugh. "There isn't one. It's infinite."

"Invent one," Aya muttered before glaring at her old caretaker. "Why are you telling them such a terrible story?"

Jeeg gave a melancholic smile accompanied by equally forlorn eyes. "I'm telling the next generation of youngsters where we come from; and well, these little planetoids are not exactly stable." His eyes met Aya's who desperately avoided their sadness. "We've been lucky to be on this beautiful planetoid for years, but nature has an odd way of giving and taking. I just wanted to prepare them for that."

Aya's voice shook in anguish, "I hope they never go through what we went through."

Jeeg was silent, contemplating what he did.

Flora slowly wobbled to her feet. Her wide eyes darted between her best friend and Jeeg before the old man amicably spoke.

"Look Aya, if it's any consolation, you jolted these old bones, so I may as well put them to use in the forest. Would that make you feel better?"

"I'm a responsible guardian," Aya says softly to herself.

"What was that?" he asks.

"I…Yes. I'd like your help."

The old man rose to his feet as the children watched him. They were filled with curiosity about the story he had told. "Well, that ends today's story time. Now this old man has to do some manual labor in spite of his aching joints."

"But what made it collapse?" One of the girls asked, paying no mind to the heated conversation that went on before.

Jeeg looked down at the girl still sitting intently, waiting for answers. "I have thought about that since the day it happened. Who or what could have caused it? I don't know. Often nature is an enigma."

The little girl sat in silence and Aya couldn't tell if she was pondering what could have happened or had no idea what 'enigma' meant.

Accompanied by Jeeg and Flora, Aya walked from the village into the nearby glade. She was hoping her job as protector would keep her mind off her past. She had lost her culture in a matter of minutes, and believed it was no one other than her who shouldered the responsibility of keeping it alive. But for one body in a vast universe, the task dwarfed a thousand planetoids.

THE BABY WYRMWOLF

Chapter 2

The forest of spirits had two kinds of trees that yielded fruit. The short, gnarled and yellow stink bushes, yielding spikey stink fruit, and the tall and elegant white wooded spirit trees that yielded tear-shaped blue and white soul fruit. The former populated most of the forest and for the colony's farmers, it was the easiest to obtain. Most of the animals avoided it because of its harsh, sharp textured skin and when opened it gave off a repugnant stench capable of knocking out the elderly, small children or those of weak constitution. It was begrudgingly the central diet for the humans of the planetoid.

The soul fruit, on the other hand, was the most desired commodity on the planetoid for both humanoids and the other animals. It hung from towering trees and when devoured it enhanced the body and mind of whoever ate it. It required twice the work and twice the danger to obtain because of its location.

Flying purple Wyrmwolves nested in the trees because the soul fruit would nourish their young while keeping them safe from harm. When farmers with wooden ladders approached the trees in hopes of scoring the fruit themselves, the hound parents would fly towards them to protect their young.

This is where Aya and Jeeg came in. They were the mediators, protecting both human and beast. Aya took this duty seriously and found great joy in it, having learned about the fragility of life and the importance of coexistence at an early age.

Aya said goodbye to Flora after her friend walked with her to the spirit forest.

Flora departed back to the village where she could remain Wyrmwolf free in her mother's tavern.

Aya met with the three members of the village council, Allons, Gully, and Myron, a fertilizer, a picker and a carpenter respectively. They were overseeing work on three separate spirit trees in their fertilizing period, but remained on standby until Aya showed up.

"Now yer the one who's late, Aya," Allons said in his thick drawl.

"Sorry, something just slowed me down," Aya tried her best to smile, "but I'm ready to protect everyone in this forest."

The red cheeked bald man, Gully, glared at her and held his hands a small distance apart. "You better do a good job. Last time I was this close to being gnawed on."

Aya flexed her arm while clutching her staff. She was utterly unphased by the man's accusations. "I can assure you, I do everything to the best of my ability, Gully."

Jeeg strolled up to the group. He stood with his head parallel to Aya's shoulder blade. "The wolves are getting restless lately. I can sense their anguish, but I don't know where it's coming from."

Myron adjusted his spectacles with a nonchalant expression. "I gathered more wood from a spirit tree recently. After that, I had to patch up some leaks for Master Du Bois."

"Oh, I didn't know you did that," Jeeg responded as Aya's face flushed in anger.

Mr. Du Bois, Flora and Jaz's father was the biggest opposition to the nature-centric ways of the elves. Myron was the only one of the three present, and since his great, great, great grandfather was the founder of the village, he exerted the biggest influence on everyone.

Aya knew Du Bois wouldn't want to prepare a whole ceremony for the destruction of a spirit tree, he just wanted to reap the benefit of its demise.

Rather than lash out, Aya flexed again and smirked. "I see Du Bois was too scared to consult me about the proper channels."

Myron raised his hands cautiously. "Now now, I'm sure Du Bois didn't mean anything by it. There's no need to discuss this anyway. We need your help, Aya. And you too, Jeeg."

"Okay," Aya dashed with great speed over to the trees. "Let's commence the gathering."

Famers grabbed their tree trunk ladders, carved meticulously out of fruitless dark wood and laid them against the trees, making sure not to jostle them too much lest awake the nearby Wyrmwolves. Some gathered burlap sacks and just as the farmer nearby Aya grabbed his sack, it twitched.

The farmer's eyes expanded and Aya quickly rushed to it, snatching it with a firm grasp and readying herself to react at any given second. Much to her relief, it was only young Jaz who had hidden himself away in the sack.

"Jaz?" Aya's eyes expressed great curiosity.

"Aww crap, you found me," he shouted as he scratched himself from being in an itchy burlap sack.

"Is that the Du Bois' kid?" The farmer jostled Aya's shoulder. Aya nodded. "Yes, and he's about to tell me why he's here."

"Well…I knew when Flora got back to town, she was going to make me do boring chores…" Jaz smiled sheepishly "and well, I'd much rather be hanging out with you. Aquans are the coolest."

Aya felt her face redden. Embarrassment was rare for her, but childhood innocence was so disarming. She debated in her head whether it would be better to take him back to Du Bois or let him watch his hero in action. Aya—though the protector of all life on the planetoid—was not above a healthy ego massage.

"Jaz, if you promise to stay by me. I won't take you back to Du Bois."

Young Jaz fist pumped the air. "Wow, you're so much cooler than my sister!"

The nearby farmer frowned in disproval but knew better than to argue with someone much larger than him. He instead grabbed a sack and began to climb the tree. "Guard me, Aya," he shouted down to her.

Aya motioned to Jaz to stand behind her as the farmer headed for the fruit hanging from the long draping rainbow leaves of the spirit tree. He shuffled it, and heard a small yipping Wyrmwolf. A much larger Wyrmwolf howled in response and began soaring around the tree with its elongated wings. It snarled and snorted from its draconic muzzle.

Aya twirled her staff before pounding it on the ground.

It began to glow from its white wood, and the white color began to extend to the tree itself.

23

The elven peacemaker smiled as the pure color began to enrapture the tree and a soothing calm fell over the yelling farmer, the baby crying and the much larger parent. The latter flew to the tree, and perched on it, watching the farmer scour the fruit like a domesticated animal.

Aya loved watching how the Wyrmwolf's demeanor changed when she soothed them. It was a satisfying feeling that resonated throughout her whole body.

"How'd you like that, little guy? Uh Jaz? Jaz?!" Aya turned around to notice that Du Bois' child was nowhere to be found.

Aya began to search around the spirit tree, until she felt a small tap on her shoulder. Turning around, she looked to see Flora clutching her heart and out of breath. "I can't believe my luck, Aya. I get back to town and all my siblings are accounted for, but stupid Jaz. Dad's going to kill me if I don't…"

Aya knew she had to own up to her friend about her missing brother. With an outward breath, Aya said, "Jaz snuck over here. He wanted to see me do my job, but it's hard to watch a child and perform at the same time."

Flora placed her hands on Aya's shoulder blades and shook her frantically. "Oh please, Aya. You need to help me. My dad already thinks I'm worthless as it is."

Aya reached her hands out to her friend's to stop them from convulsing. "Gotcha. I don't like old crimson suspenders either, so I'll be happy to help you prove him wrong."

"Thanks, my friend." Flora sighed. "Let's just get this over with. The spirit woods give me the jitters."

24

Aya alerted everyone about the missing child; the farmers ceased from their harvest as a result. Everyone had a mutual consideration for Jaz, partially because they cared for him, but more importantly his heritage would allow them to gain the favor of the house of Du Bois.

They moved around the forest, checking every stink bush and spirit tree they harvested from, but success had not dawned on them. As Aya and Flora paced around the same grove of trees, Flora began to whimper and tremble. "I just realized something, Aya. What if he went…there?"

Aya's long ears twitched. "You think he went to the Hallow? Why would he go there?"

"He always bragged and said when he got older, he'd pick the finest soul fruit in the forest. You know where that grows, right?"

"The Matriarch tree," Aya responded immediately.

The two said no more and headed back to the harvest area where the three leaders stood with Jeeg. A much taller man with neatly combed ginger hair gelled up with spirit tree sap, and an equally orderly mustache, stood with them. His hands were crossed and he looked upon everyone with distain. The three leaders cowered in fear over this man with his dapper suit and suspenders.

"Flora, Aya. I hope you know that my son is not accounted for," said the man with a caustic voice. "And by the words of these men, it is your fault."

Aya glared at Jeeg who put his hands up in the air and then pointed at a bush. "Don't look at me. I was sleeping peacefully when these fellows woke me up," the old man responded.

"Dad, I'm so sorry," Flora carried on. "I was just heading back to town when I found out Jaz was gone."

"You had one job, Flora," Du Bois said with a scowl, "and it's much less difficult than the one these men have. You have no excuse to be slacking." Du Bois turned to Aya. "And you, earian, I wish you'd stop hanging around my daughter. She's getting infected with your lax attitude and disregard for danger."

Aya pursed her lips like she had devoured a mouthful of stink fruit. Aya absolutely loathed when she was called an earian. It was something people started calling her and Jeeg when they first came to the planet. For prejudiced people, her ears were a point of mockery, but to her they were a symbol of pride. She bit her tongue, wishing to honor Jeeg who had long convinced Du Bois' father to somewhat honor nature, and instead spoke up in defense of Flora.

She knew that Flora was heading to retrieve Jaz before her stress disorder was triggered by the baby Wyrmwolf. Mr. Du Bois only ever saw what he wanted to see. If it didn't align with his view point, he disregarded it completely.

"Please don't take it out on her," said Aya. "We know where Jaz is and we're going to retrieve him."

"We do?" Flora asked.

"Shhh," Aya said, "He's at the Matriarch Tree. Let's all go right now and instead of wasting away time with this game of blame."

The trio of leaders, Jeeg, Flora, Du Bois and Aya all made a b-line to the Hallow where the Matriarch tree stood tall. Its trunk was white with blue swirls formed around its large knotted burls resulting from immense age and stress. They formed stepping platforms that twisted and turned around the tree, allowing even a child to gain leverage when climbing them. Despite the danger, this tree was the perfect playground for a young adventurer like Jaz.

Everyone scanned the rainbow leaves of the beautiful and ancient tree, hoping to find the child. They called out to him. "Jaz! Jaz!"

"Listen, do you hear that?" Aya asked.

"We don't have ears the size of the Wyrmwolf's ears," Gully muttered under his breath.

Aya disregarded him. "I hear the breathing of a small child. It's coming from above us." She dashed to the knots in the tree and quickly leapt from one to another, traveling up the towering trunk at a fast rate. She did not slip once; as a youthful Aquan she had greater coordination than a human. She reached the branches and looked down to see everyone watching her.

The nimble girl gave a confident smile, looking down on them and quickly noticed the contents on the large rainbow palm leaves. Her smile softened as she saw the young boy sleeping in the trees alongside a large blue soul fruit, and to her surprise, a silver Wyrmwolf pup. Both were equally young and docile, with Jaz resting his head on the creature's soft furry body.

Aya sighed and dreamed that this could be the relationship between humans and all animals.

She didn't want to wake them so she slowly inched herself along the palm leaves. She aimed to do it fast since she had no idea if the palm leaves could support her large body like it held the two tiny ones. She moved in on her knees and stretched her long arms out to grab the boy. When she laid her hands on him, his eyes shot open and he let out the loudest scream.

Aya flinched and her body cracked the branch. She quickly yanked Jaz into her arms and as the branch fell forward, she leapt to the closest burl with the boy hanging from her shirt.

Jaz was still screaming, but Aya tried to soothe him "Jaz, it's me. What were you doing up there?"

The boy's chest convulsed and he was clearly out of breath from yelling. He spoke in short sharp bursts. "Aya…I wanted…to…get…a spirit fruit…for you…but I was so tired from climbing…I fell asleep…with…my new friend." Jaz looked down at the cracked branch and gasped. "My friend…"

Aya quickly leaped down the burls with Jaz in tow and she ran to where the branch had fallen. Everyone gathered around them.

Mr. Du Bois was the first to talk. He towered over young Jaz, who shuddered in his presence. "I heard why you were up there." Without the subtlety of a man dressed as dapper as himself, Du Bois slapped Jaz. "Listen to me next time I forbid you to do something. All of my rules are for your own good, you stupid girl."

Jaz looked like he was about to cry, but he instead sped away from Mr. Du Bois and ran towards the downed branches. Tears began to roll down his face as he looked upon the injured Wyrmwolf. "My friend."

Everyone followed Jaz around the branch and saw the Wyrmwolf softly crying as blood soaked its fur. Allons gently chimed in. "I've never seen a beastie like that before. Them baby Wyrmwolves are usually pink."

Aya and Jeeg ran to accompany Jaz as he crouched beside the animal.

Jeeg softly spoke to the boy, "That's the elder Wyrmwolf's child, the future matriarch, and it looks like she's in pretty bad shape. She is stronger than she looks. Though dormant now, this child is from the ancient Wyrmwolf goddess. Her soul possesses the wisdom, strength and influence of all her ancestors. Forever reincarnating, her soul is tethered to this planetoid, bound by an eternal duty to guard her people and her land."

Jaz cried to Jeeg. "I don't care about your stories! Is there anything we can do for her?"

Jeeg rubbed his goatee and closed his eyes. He then reached for the downed soul fruit and a rainbow palm leaf. He used the leaf to wrap the cut the creature was enduring, and whipped out a small knife before dicing the fruit open with precision. The elderly Aquan then placed a small piece inside the creature's whining maw. "The best thing for recovery is nourishment and proper medical treatment."

Jaz nodded his head in agreement. "Please, heal her with your magic." Jaz's tiny voice was interrupted by a loud snarl from the sky.

Everyone looked up and saw the shadow of a large beast blot out the sun. They were twice the size of the average Wyrmwolf, with mossy green white fur and two scars across their eyes.

"The elder Wyrmwolf!" Jeeg exclaimed.

The elder spread their lengthy white wings and took a dive over the crowd of people.

29

Everyone ducked, diving into the grass to avoid the incoming attack.

"Is everyone okay?" Allons asked after everyone rose up.

Flora began to take a head count. "I think so…wait, where's Jaz?"

Everyone looked to the attacking beast and saw the small boy saw hanging from its mouth.

"Jaz!" Flora yelled.

The boy hung from his shirt and began to scream loudly, but his words were incomprehensible and terrified. The beast took to the sky, and began to head towards a mountain further past the soul tree.

"Where is he taking my brother?" Flora asked, about to have another panic attack.

Jeeg shook his head. "Did you see her eyes? Her vision is damaged and she may have mistaken your brother for her child."

Aya grimaced and kicked the ground, looking away from everyone else. She blamed herself for Jaz's kidnapping and the injuries caused to the Wyrmwolf baby. She knew in her heart she had to put her guilt aside and focus on righting the wrongs she had caused.

THE ELDER'S WRATH

Chapter 3

Evening shaded the town in orange as dark clouds rolled over the horizon.

Aya had spent hours comforting her best friend, but it was to no avail. She herself felt uncomfortable just standing around, but she had taken Jeeg's advice to wait until the town came up with a unanimous answer to dealing with the elder Wyrmwolf and Jaz's abduction.

Aya leaned against the soft cotton bed in Flora's room. The room's owner paced back and forth, carefully lifting her dress so she would not trip over it in the midst of her frantic episode. "My lord. This is probably the worst thing that could happen," she said in her high and wavering voice.

Aya looked around. The neat order of everything was betrayed her friend's emotionally frayed disposition. She looked at a large painting that hung parallel to the bedroom. In watercolor, the Du Bois family was depicted. Mr. and Mrs. Du Bois stood with Flora, the father in his formal wear and the mother in a large frilly pink dress. Flora was the third tallest in her large floppy hat that mirrored her mother's. The children stood below them all in a line, two brothers in their early teens, two sisters in their pre-teens and Jaz, the youngest of them all.

At first it was just Flora, but Du Bois wanted to make his children plentiful so his blood could run the planetoid.

"Flor, it's okay," Aya said, trying to gently talk to her friend so she wouldn't have a conniption. "Just know that it's more my fault than yours."

Flora turned around from pacing to face Aya with pain-stricken eyes. "Is it though? My father is right. I barely have any responsibilities and yet I still ruin them!"

"You have the hardest job of all, Flor." Aya nodded. "Animals are a lot easier to look after; human children are far fussier and more selfish. I mean we're all animals, but humans seem to have forgotten that."

"I need to take my mind off this." Flora paced over to her sewing table where a needle, coal iron and scissors laid next to a hooded poncho draped over a majority of the table. Reaching for the needle Flora began to work on the rather complex pattern embroidered into it from the chest to the fringed bottom. The pattern constituted of a colorful figure dressed in blue and green with elfin ears. A circle surrounded each figure, representing a bubble. This was the primary magic power of the Aquans, Aya's people.

Flora had nearly finished the whole thing, as the patterns had reached the bottom with a few more figures to go. She observed a small piece of cloth separate from the poncho with similar patterns that were woven more expertly than hers. Frantically, she began to thread as Aya calmly walked over to her table.

"I'll still remember how I first met you, Flor." Aya smiled softly and her normally commanding voice grew relaxed and mild. "Everyone stared at Jeeg and I when we first came to this planetoid, but you said…"

As she embroidered, Flora managed a sweet smile back. "Those clothes are so cool and pretty! I've never seen anything like it!"

Aya nodded in agreement. "And as a future seamstress, you wanted to know how to make them."

Flora gave a tense laugh, her nervousness seeped through as hard as her as she tried to restrain it. "Haha…yeah."

Aya walked closer to her friend and leaned on the poncho with a smile. "You know, I came to realize over the years how much that meant to me…for you to keep our tradition alive."

"Even if I can't match the skill of an Aquan seamstress?" said Flora, ceasing her sewing to hear her friend's answer.

"None of them are making clothing anymore," Aya said with a gentle sadness. "This means the whole planetoid to me, Flor."

"Well…I do say," Flora gave another smile back and her cheeks turned crimson, "I'm glad I can make something to honor them and you."

"I truly feel honored." Aya began to lift the poncho and feel its soft texture. A sly look crept onto her elfish Aquan face. "Can I use this? I know you're not finished, but I think I'm going to need it."

"Why?" Flora's eyes illuminated with questions.

"My ears, they're very sensitive to humidity." Aya pointed to them. "It's going to rain soon, and I need to get going."

"Where are you going?" Flora's eyes expanded as they often did.

Before Aya could answer, Flora's mother, the spitting image of her daughter in aged bony flesh spoke stood in the doorway. Her face was full of terror as lightning crashed through the sky. "Flora, dear, your father. He won't listen to me."

"What is this about?" Aya asked on her friend's behalf.

"He's outside in the town square right now and he says he's going into the spirit woods to find Jaz." The middle-aged woman grasped her heart. "He's been telling the villagers he'll stab the beast right through its heart in order to get back his son."

Flora's mother walked into the room and stood before her. Her long hoop skirt was soaked from the oncoming rain and her hat hung soaked over her head. Her long hair remained dry for the most part, indicating that the hat had done its work. "Please Flora, you're the oldest. Tell him he can't take on a monster like that."

Flora held her head as low as her stitched patterns. "Dad likes me least of all. He blames me for all that's happened to Jaz. I doubt he'll listen to me."

Aya put her hand on her friend's shoulder. "Flor, like I said, it's my fault. I take full responsibility for what has happened." Aya pointed to the poncho. "Please, give this to me."

"Oh, alright." Flora lifted up the poncho, with a few Aquan symbols missing, and handed it to Aya, who slipped it over her midriff and her long, toned, and slender muscled arms. It fit perfectly over her fit body, hanging just below her cargo shorts.

Just as the elf was getting adjusted to her clothes, Mrs. Du Bois raised her voice. "Aya what are you planning to do?"

Aya pulled up the hood on her Aquan poncho. "I'm going to bring Jaz back. No one will have to die."

"You can't just go out in this storm!" Mrs. Du Bois shouted at her. "I care about your life too, Aya. The village needs you. We all do. Don't be reckless!"

Aya began to walk away. "I'm responsible for what happened today, Mrs. Du Bois. That's the absolute truth. And when an Aquan is wrong, they fix their mistakes no matter what it takes." She turned around with a glare of passionate fire and a commanding voice to match it. "I'm not going to allow harm to come to a mother who was just protecting her child. And I won't allow any harm to come to Jaz. Oh, I'll protect your husband too if it comes to it."

Mrs. Dubois fans herself, unsure what to say.

Flora raised her voice for the first time since she sat down, "Please Aya, I don't want you to risk your life like this either. Mother is right."

Aya immediately changed her tone from passionately harsh to gentle and considerate. "Flor, no one's going to get hurt. I'm a protector and a mediator. I will reach an understanding with the elder Wyrmwolf."

The elven warrior raised her soul staff in triumph. "I'm going to get to the root of all of this. Thanks for the poncho, Flor." She waved farewell to her friend before slamming the door, accompanied by a blinding crash of thunder and lighting. Walking down stairs and out of the Du Bois manor, she could still hear Mrs. Du Bois shouting. "Be careful Aya, I hear the Noctursa are extra ravenous and dangerous these days."

Once she set foot outside, Aya stamped her staff. A dome of rain water formed above her, shielding her from the deluge. Her ability to manipulate water allowed an Aquan granted her many conveniences that others were bereft of.

She advanced to the center of the town where the fruit hoister was. It was a long pole with a rope, securing a large net of soul fruit at the top.

Soul Fruit was best left exposed to the light of the planetoid's tiny moons, but the ongoing threat of a ravenous Noctursa meant they should be secured and out of reach. For someone who was seasoned by the aerobics of her tribe, these fruits were easily obtainable.

Aya dove into the levitating ball of water she generated with her staff and rode in the bubble up to the net. She reached through the bubble, squeezing a fruit through one of the air holes in the net. Staring at the fruit as it shimmered in the moonlight, Aya began to salivate. She dropped down quickly with her bubble splashing all around her. She scanned her surroundings but found nothing of note. Du Bois had already left town and made haste into the woods and so Aya did the same.

Seeking shelter under a small Atma tree at the foot of the forest, she scarfed down the moon-charged soul fruit. This mission required both speed and endurance, which meant it required fruity enhancements. She especially needed the power of the fruit since she intended to scale the white mountain in a single night. Reaching the mountain alone was half the challenge because of the nocturnal foraging patterns of the night bears. If what Mrs. Du Bois had said was true, something had made them tense and extra ravenous.

"Just my kind of challenge," Aya said under her breath. She could feel power surge through her muscles as she bit the fruit, making her body convulse and glow slightly blue as her metabolism sped up. In a split second, she tore through the trees running on the tops of her feet in order to be move silently.

Sudden growling made her stop and take shelter behind a tree. She peered out and spotted a Noctursa. The dark and burly creature was the size of the small cabins in her village. Blue markings shone under the bear's fur. They resembled tattoos of some form of ancient calligraphy unknown to her. These neon blue bear tats were illuminated by the moonlight-enhanced soul fruit.

The nocturnal bear surveyed the landscape with equally blue eyes, bending down to sniff the air as rain poured overhead, matting their fur and making it smell musty.

Aya slid up against the tree, her long body twisting and turning to match the way the tree stood. She leaned her head out from behind the tree and quickly peeked out.

The bear grunted and reached towards the Atma tree, but before she was found out, the bear stopped. They stood upright and began to swat at the air almost in a drunken stupor.

Aya squinted hard, trying to see what the Noctursa was fighting. It looked like nothing; but faintly shining through the pouring rain, Aya noticed a light.

Lighting flashed and the tiny light exploded into a Wyrmwolf made entirely out of spectral green light. It hovered in front of the bear to let out a ghostly howl as a warning before zooming through the Noctursa, making the dark bear turn a ghostly pale. With a shiver, the lumbering giant moaned and lumbered off into the forest.

"I guess even Noctursa fear ghosts," Aya muttered with a disbelieving expression. The ghostly figure of the Wyrmwolf zoomed off and Aya followed, heading towards the mountain.

Sensing an uneasy presence during her pursuit, Aya decided to investigate. She smelled the raw fire of burning wood and, using her acute sense of smell, she tracked down the source of it. She headed deeper and deeper into the hollow. When she arrived at the center, she gasped in horror.

The Matriarch tree, the one that had been flourishing several hours earlier, had been demolished. Torn and twisted, fragments of wood and fire burned everywhere as it had collapsed. She could smell the ash that had spread all the way to the sky above through the humidity. She could also feel the humid air grow cold as more spectral Wyrmwolves appeared around her.

"This is horrendous…" she stifled out.

Aya trembled to her knees and prayed for the great tree. She reflected on the centuries it had lasted until this tragic night.

Memories came flooding back to when she would voyage there as a child and play with Jeeg.

Shaking her head, Aya quickly leapt to her feet. She knew there was no time for sentimentality. She ran further past the downed tree, knowing there was no way she could soothe the spiritual unrest alone.

Soon she arrived at the foot of the white mountain.

The Aquan warrior knew a quarter of her stamina was depleted, so she had to be careful when using a bubble to carry her to the ensuing confrontation. With a sparkling silver movement of her diamond fish tattoos, she expanded the watery shield she had created over her head to become a bubble. The rain was pouring down on all sides and she leapt, merging with her bubble. She began to concentrate and ascend with her eyes closed.

Having taken a deep breath, she meditated with her legs crossed inside the water bubble as it flew toward the peak of the mountain. She knew any break in concentration would lead her to fall to her death. It was hard enough to know when and where to release, but she kept one eye open and focused on the cliff.

As she ascended higher and higher, she began to feel ice across her bubble. The rain in the darkened night sky had become bits of hail. Another crash occurred, and Aya could feel the same uncomfortable presence around her again.

A visible streak of lighting lit the sky, and Aya found herself face to face with a spectral Wyrmwolf. It shrieked like a murdered animal and flew through her bubble and into her.

As she lost her concentration, the water around her dissipated, and it was only her enhanced reflexes that allowed her to react in seconds. Jamming her staff in a hole between two rocks on the side of a crag, her life hung on a single piece of wood as she gripped it tightly.

The staff began to bend as Aya moved across it with tense, subtle hand movements and even tenser breath. Aya looked further up, seeing the bluff was a short distance from her. She bent the staff down further,

39

and then with all of her strength invested, took a single leap up. After grabbing her staff with her feet, she sprang forth, grasping the cliff with the edges of two fingers. Her strength was beginning to leave her, but with a swift swing of her staff by her feet, she had created another water bubble to raise her back to the top of the cliff.

She dropped out of her bubble and fell to the ground. Breathing desperately like a fish stranded on dry land, she rose from her knees on the muddy ground. She had come to a cave that seemed to tunnel through the mountain. The stone white mountain was etched with dark paint, or perhaps blood.

Aya worried it could be Jaz's blood, but thankfully it looked like it had been there for a very long time. The blood or paint was etched into small humanoid figures, cave drawings from times long passed. Aya had little time to ponder them. Her priority was finding Jaz.

She exhaled and observed the altitude. Up on the mountain, thunder and lightning battled each other with great intensity. The moons shone red through the darkened sky and endlessly pouring rain and hail.

Aya heard a roar from above. The dragon-like Wyrmwolf descended upon the bluff, flying at Aya with her teeth strewn maw. The projectile beast missed her by a head.

The elder landed, lacking the grace a winged animal normally harbored. Her legs scattered and limped before crashing down into the muddy gravel with a sickly growl.

Aya gave a dutiful bow before speaking. "Oh, great elder Wyrmwolf. Please allow my presence."

She looked over the creature as it gathered itself. Her majestic wing span was torn. It was unbelievable how she could still fly. Brutal scratches were cut into her body. The ancient markings glowed brightly in spite of the rain and darkness. The creature turned and gave an intense glare from its injured eyes. They pierced Aya even if they could no longer see clearly.

The beast spoke with a voice brutish and primal, yet feminine and motherly. "Spare me this reverent nonsense, Aquan. If it wasn't for your human friends, my child would be beside me."

Aya touched her own cold face in shock. "How can you speak to me, great one?"

The creature continued to glare through Aya. "I can barely see you, but I know you are a naïve child. Your ancestors could commune with the forest elders, you fool."

"My ancestors?" Aya's voice drew higher. "But I'm not from here."

"The Aquans, Sylphens and Acridians were a nomadic race and lived on many planetoids." The elders voice grew spiteful. "They were caretakers, but they were driven out by those wretched humans."

Aya took a step back in shock. The rain soaking her clothes added to the feeling of heaviness.

The Wyrmwolf took a step in Aya's direction. Her mouth hung open, growling while bits of foam and blood seeped from her maw. She lowered her head and lunged at Aya, but the Aquan's reflexes allowed her to swiftly roll.

The beast's wings spread open and she flew at Aya again. Her mouth opened wide in an attempt to crush the invader's face. Aya remembered

41

Jeeg's words as she swiveled away: "A Wyrmwolf never backs down in a fight against a perceived foe. They are not creatures of flight, contrary to their wings."

"I don't want to fight you, oh great one!" Aya shouted reverently.

The elder Wyrmwolf shook her head in disdain. "I will not take formalities from a fiend who assisted in taking my child away!" The beast opened her mouth wide, and expelled a frosty wind. The wind transformed the soggy ground to ice, and raindrops into snowflakes.

Aya gasped when she found her clothes ensnared in ice. She banged at the ice with her staff before remembering the powers she held in her hand. She took a moment to breath in and concentrate.

Aya closed her eyes and raised her staff, beginning to focus her soul into it. "I know you're wounded, elder Wyrmwolf. But the place you're hurt deepest is your grand spirit and it's making you irrational." Aya grimaced as she felt the elder's jaws clamp down on her arm.

"You robbed a blind woman of her child," cried the beast in a disarmingly feminine way.

Aya ignored her and continued to focus. The pain was intensifying, but she quickly removed her energy body from that part of her body, numbing it. "Be at ease." Aya's eyes locked with the Wyrmwolf's damaged sockets. The creature's chest began to convulse less and less. "My mentor Jeeg, an Aquan caretaker, he is tending to your child's wounds." Aya's voice though mellow remained commanding as well. "We are protectors of all of nature, including humans. We will do all we can to prevent harm of either for as long as we live."

The Wyrmwolf's jaws began to relax on Aya's arms. The creature's eyes closed gently. "The wood of an Atma tree," said the beast, breathing out. "Its properties are the very essence of life itself. Only someone in tune with the energies of nature would be able to wield one."

"I'm nowhere as close to the big dream as you." Aya's face began to drip with tears, meshing with the rain. "I only know what's precious because of what I lost." Aya turned away. "And I look down on those who squander what I've lost."

The Wyrmwolf's face, though built in a permanent scowl, softened through her eyes. "Are you speaking of the human child who was with me?"

"I don't want to lose anyone else." Aya rubbed her eyes.

The beast looked down as the rain pounded on her. "That child was so scared; she leapt off the mountain to the trees below. I don't know what became of that little thing."

Aya grimaced and walked to the edge of the cliff to gaze at the forest beneath them. The emotional pain and adrenaline had numbed her bleeding. She didn't blame the Wyrmwolf or Jaz for what happened, but grief emanated through her nonetheless. "Jaz is lost." She put her hands together but struggled to chant. Her tears overwhelmed her.

The elder Wyrmwolf howled as she fell to the ground in a heap of matted, soggy fur. Aya turned around and ran to the beast's aid.

"My injuries," the elder growled "They're finally doing me in."

"Who...who did this to you?" Aya asked, resting her hand on the creature's body with tears streaming down her cheeks.

"Something slashed my eyes and separated me from child in the process. I didn't see who or what this monster was, but they had enough speed that they could get away with it."

Aya gazed at the forest guardian's dulled eyes and followed the injuries onto the giant slash marks on her body.

The elder struggled to keep still as she tried to rise to her feet. "As I was searching for my pup, a Noctursa came between me. With my eyes in such a state and my soul torn, I could barely fight back."

Aya looked pained. "That's cruel. That Noctursa shouldn't have disrespected you like that."

"I harbor no resentment. She was defending her own child," the elder responded. "What parent wouldn't want to bring absolute destruction onto whatsoever threatened their dear one." In a sad, resigned voice the elder added, "Whether they be Wyrmwolves, Noctursa or even humans."

The beast howled to the heavens as it spilled out its tears. "Please, I just want to see my daughter again."

Aya rose from her crouched position. "Can you fly? I'll take you to her."

The elder followed suit, rising from where she had fallen. "I will give it my all."

Aya, with tentative movement, approached the great white beast and climbed upon her back.

The Wyrmwolf snarled. "Normally I'd tear you limb from limb for daring to sit upon me," the proud beast's voice grew coarse "but my daughter is all I have left."

Aya gripped the Wyrmwolf's rain drenched fur, leaning forward as the beast began to charge towards the precipice. She knew it was too late for Jaz. There was no way he could have survived the dangers of this place. There was nothing she could do to help the dead, but as long as life remained in the elder, she was determined to do all she could to help the suffering mother. She wished she could have something for Jaz and her friends and family back on her home planet in their last moments…but she was powerless. Aya bowed her head in lament as the Wyrmwolf spread her wings for what may have been the very last time.

THE SPIRIT PACT

Chapter 4

Aya and the great elder struggled against the forces of nature. Rain, wind and hail battered them as they rode through the night sky. Quick intervals between the flashes of lightning and crashes of thunder indicated the storm was still close. Aya held her staff at her side, her fear of losing her balance prevented her from sitting upright and blocking the rain. Aya pressed her face into the Wyrmwolf's furry neck.

"Aquan, are you all right?" The elder asked.

"I've just…" Aya tried to speak, but the lump in her stomach prevented it for a moment "I've never ridden a Wyrmwolf before. And this storm is fearsome."

"I've never had anyone on my back before," the Wyrmwolf grunted back. "I'm growing weaker by the moment. Are we close by? I'm feeling your weight more and more."

Aya was silent until the Wyrmwolf raised her head and spoke again. "Aquan, can you see where the village is?"

Aya pulled the Wyrmwolf's hair in order to prop herself up on her head. She panned the skies, squinting from the heavy rain drops splattering across her face until she saw the fire lights from the village cabins a short distance away. "It's not that far. just keep flying straight."

"Tell me when you want me to descend. I'm not some domesticated steed," The Wyrmwolf told Aya briskly.

Aya stared towards the horizon with great intensity. She hoped this long tempestuous night would come to a gentle end. But in harsh irony, the sky lit up like an explosion and lightning struck the elder and Aya.

The beast erupted in fire with a loud howl, causing Aya to fall backwards alongside her animal companion.

Aya began to lose consciousness as she fell. She could still see the rainbow palms below, darkened in the abyss of night. Soon, her vision was consumed with darkness and Aya could no longer tell if she was dead or alive. Her mind was adrift in the vastness of her subconscious.

The sound of overhead birds and something scraping the ground woke Aya with a startle. She gazed at the atmosphere above her. The sky was bright blue and the great star warmed the ground along with Aya's dirt encrusted face.

She found herself lying face up in slowly drying mud with an Atma tree's rainbow leaves scattered around her. Extending her hand, she picked up one of the colorful palm leaves.

"Must've broke my fall," she muttered, holding the leaf above her to inspect. "Thank the ancients." She heard more scraping sounds and rose to find their source.

Several feet away Aya could see the elder Wyrmwolf's body crumpled in the mud, slowly inching her way across the floor of the forest.

Aya crawled to her feet with grogginess, stumbling over to the elder. As she made her way, she glanced to the left and saw her staff lying adjacent from them. She quickly grasped it and moved to the elder's aid.

"Elder!" Aya cried.

Aya observed the state of the Wyrmwolf. Her wings were completely broken, and her eyes were distant and empty. The beast slouched, hanging limp and Aya could tell there were signs of a stroke. In spite of this, she kept on crawling.

"I…need…to…reach… my child," the beast croaked from its hanging jaw.

Tears seeped from Aya's eyes and she held her hands in front of her face. "Please…there must be something I can do for you. Can I use my staff?"

"Save your energy," the Wyrmwolf groaned, "And I am much too heavy to be lifted."

Aya frowned through her tears. "Please, if there's any way to assist you. Any way at all…please let me."

The Wyrmwolf barely moved or batted an eye. All her glorious vitality had abandoned her.

"Elder…elder please don't be dead. Elder?"

The beast's bloody eye slowly slid towards Aya and her maw slowly opened and closed. "I'm just…thinking."

"What are you thinking about?"

"Will you listen to an old woman ruminate about her life?" The beast asked in the slightest deadpan.

Aya crouched down beside the elder.

The forest guardian spoke slowly, but with a passionate creak. "Shortly after I was born, I learned I was different from all the

Wyrmwolf pups. I learned my life was not my own. I was forced to uphold a sacred duty to the world I lived in."

"Your fur…" Aya said quietly, "does it designate that?"

"It's not the fur that designates my rank," the elder explained, "It's the transfer of power from one to another. During the creation of this planetoid, the creator bestowed the title of guardian onto three beasts, the Thunderboar, Wyrmwolf and Noctursa. My father was a descendent of the chosen Wyrmwolf."

"So, each of the three tribes have a guardian among their ranks?" Aya responded quickly.

"Yes, they do," the knowledgeable beast continued, "and they have kept the power to their lineages for centuries. These three ancient beasts protect Nature's Gate and have done so proudly."

"Nature's Gate?" Aya's eyes went wide. "The gate that protects the center of the planetoid?"

"Yes, child." The Wyrmwolf refrained from speaking to continue ruminating further. At last, she spoke with grave sincerity. "I needed to reach my daughter in order to transfer my powers before I pass on, or the world as we know it will become highly unstable."

"What will happen?" Aya asked.

"Nature's Gate will open, and anyone will be able to enter." The beast reflected again before speaking. "My assailant might have been attempting to gain access to Nature's Gate."

Aya put her arms around the Wyrmwolf, deeply distraught. "I'll never let them do it. You have my word as an Aquan that I'll do anything to help."

"Anything?" The Wyrmwolf craned her neck towards the determined child.

"Yes, anything." Aya said, nodding frantically before her head came to a stop.

Even in a near death state, the Wyrmwolf still retained dignity in her voice. She knew the gravity of the situation required total premeditation, even if her brain and body were failing. "Give me your hand, the hand I bit."

Aya slowly moved her hand toward the Wyrmwolf. She had never performed this ritual before, and even if the matters were grave and required, her youthful mind still had fear of what would happen next.

"Place it in my mouth," the elder ordered. "Do it now."

Aya stuck her hand right between the elder's limp jaws. She observed her wrist which had fang marks and dry blood from when she was last attacked.

"Do not be afraid," the elder responded, "You are performing a great duty. Something only Aquans, Sylphens and Acridians can do."

Aya slowly opened her eyes. She gazed right at the wolf's jaw. Feeling the pride from her deceased race, she no longer allowed fear to permeate her. "I know that my soul will never reach paradise, but this Planetoid…it is my paradise. It shall be my responsibility for all of time. I'm ready, great one," she said with a firm and unwavering tone.

The elder's jaw swung forward, burying itself into Aya's hand. At first, Aya only felt the pain, but slowly she began to feel something blissful manifesting within her.

Aya felt a oneness with the elder, an existence of two minds coming together into one.

A connection into the Wyrmwolf's mind gave her a brand-new perspective. She let out a sharp cry; it sounded more like a howl, and she buckled to her knees.

Ancient energy coursed through Aya's body and her senses heightened. Her already powerful sense of smell and hearing, became canine-like, and she envisioned a ceremony of howling elders bestowing these powers onto her. When she opened her eyes, the euphoric sensation had left her lying on the ground, bent in prayer.

Rising to her feet, she looked around and noticed that the elder Wyrmwolf was nowhere to be found.

Aya cried out to the forest and animals who surrounded her. "What has become of you, oh great guardian?"

"Do not worry, child," a familiar motherly voice spoke from below.

Aya held her wrist to her face and noticed a brand-new tattoo inked into her formerly injured arm. It was a tribal image of a Wyrmwolf, and Aya's eyes bugged out as she saw it speak in an animated way.

"When the elder's life is done and the power is passed on, the elder can choose to become a spiritual guide for the next in line. They can choose..."

Aya let out a scream and shook her hand frantically, "Have I gone crazy? I didn't choose anything."

"I suppose your subconscious did," the elder said with a chuckle before her face turned grave from sudden thoughts. "I have broken our lineage in order to pass my powers onto you."

Aya's mind drew a complete blank from her many flustering thoughts, so the elder spoke again in a reassured voice. "But do not worry about the old lineages. I had a feeling my child, a frail pup, might not have been able to handle the demands of being a guardian."

The Wyrmwolf tattoo gave a smile. "Thanks to you my child can live without her mother's burden. All that power and responsibility is now something you must shoulder."

Aya nodded silently and walked over to the nearby Atma tree. She leaned up against it cross-legged. She felt the heat of the great star beginning to warm everything over. She began to sweat in her muddy poncho and before long, she had shed it. She gazed at the patterns now stained and murky, and the threads unraveled in several places. She hoped Flora could mend it.

"What's wrong, Aya?" The elder asked as Aya tentatively twirled a loose string on it.

"Can I really guard the gate if I couldn't even save Jaz?" Aya cried in angst before processing what her new tattoo said. "Aya? You called me by my name."

The inked Wyrmwolf looked up at Aya with a placid look on her face. "This isn't the first time I've heard of you and Jeeg, Members of our tribe sing praise about your dedication and concern for others. I was not so easily swayed."

"Glad someone's appreciative," Aya muttered in response. "We have no trouble calming beasts of all kin, it's humans we have trouble reasoning with."

"I believe you can succeed in this great struggle between animals, elves and humans," the Wyrmwolf said calmly. "You got through to me and I'm as stubborn as a rock tree."

Aya managed a small smile from the flattery. Her aqua blue eyes sparkled in the sunlight for the first time. "Now that I have you to guide me, great elder, I can certainly try."

The Wyrmwolf frowned, "Enough with the pompous great elder nonsense. You and Jeeg are all the same. It's always I'm not worthy or some other incessant form of groveling." She snarls. "My name is Eterna. Had you introduced yourself earlier, I would have said so sooner. I have enough respect for myself to not utter my true name to one without proper etiquette."

Aya gave a kind glance. "It's my honor to meet you Eterna."

"Honor?"

"It's a pleasure to meet you." Aya grins.

"Good girl," Eterna nodded. "Was that so hard, child? If I had to hear 'great elder' again, I'd liken being under your skin to purgatory."

Aya gave a small smile and stood up, toting her poncho and staff. She headed back to town without a word. Even if her newfound partnership with Eterna had brightened her mood a little, many things weighed heavy on her brain and a whole array of emotions flashed through her young mind.

The Aquan was admittedly fascinated with her new ties to nature in spite of her trepidation of being the new guardian of the planetoid. But what overwhelmed her was the deep sadness of Jaz's death. She would still have to break the news to the Du Bois family. With a heavy heart, she approached the village, ready to be the bearer of the grave news.

She glanced into the distance and saw a group of people standing around town. She wondered what the hubbub was, and as she got closer, she saw why.

Her heart fluttered with joy as she saw Jaz standing at the center of a sea of smiling faces. Aya grinned with a face full of tears.

He was alive.

Du Bois stood at the center too, his arm bandaged in a sling, but with an equally broad grin under his orange mustache. A hand landed on Jaz's head and ruffled his hair.

Aya followed the hand up to the mysterious man it belonged to. He was brown skinned with long flowing hair, his face chiseled but smooth and he had dark harrowing eyes that tickled her curiosity.

Aya had never seen someone else with darker skin, even a human and her curiosity outweighed her cautious nature. When he caught wind of her, his self-confident facial expression changed to one of surprise, like he was revisiting an unexpected memory.

Aya took notice of what he held in his hands. It was a helmet. It was reflective and dark, with small slits for eyes and large tubes where the mouth was. Aya realized at that moment, this man was from another world.

VISITOR FROM THE STARS

Chapter 5

Aya found herself so transfixed on the visitor so she didn't notice when Flora ran in and embraced her.

"Thank every star in the sky," Flora cried covering her friend's neck with her long curly hair.

Shocked, Aya slowly put her hand around her friends back.

"It's a miracle times two. Some man found Jaz and my father in the forest and now we've found you too," she continued as Aya smiled and patted her friend's back in order to calm her down.

"Who is he?" Aya asked as she peered around Flora's floppy hat before looking at her friend again.

Flora positioned her large eyes towards the heavens. "He says he came from outer space," she frowned in confusion. "Funny place to live. I didn't think you could breathe up there."

Aya gave a friendly roll of her eyes. "I don't think he literally lives in space. He came from another planetoid. There are countless little worlds out there."

With a flash of her eyes, Aya moved towards the crowd of farmers. The most prominent member being Mrs. Du Bois. She stood with her hands placed firmly on her returned son's shoulder and her other hand on her husband's good shoulder. Accompanying her were several blushing wives of the farmers, who were gazing longingly at the space traveler as their husbands tried their best not to feel inferior.

The traveler went back to pretending he hadn't noticed Aya since they first locked eyes, but then turned back to her with more reserved expression. He looked over her shapely, toned figure. The space tourist spoke in a voice that was rough and deep, but at the same time had a boyish charm to it. "Whoa, you didn't tell me you had women like her on your planet!"

"What's that supposed to mean?" One of the women in the crowd jeered as the space-man strolled over to Aya.

"Hello, foxy lady," the man said, inserting his left hand into his jacket pocket, but keeping his thumb visible.

Aya felt her ears grow warm. They were always the most sensitive part of her body. "Nice to meet a man who appreciates my foxlike tracking abilities," she said with a bashful smile.

She looked down and saw Eterna glaring up at her. "Child, he is leering at you. I've been around long enough to hear the entire dictionary of mating calls."

Aya shook her head and glared at the man who remained confident and smug, not having heard Eterna. He was unflinching in the face of a towering Aquan and his height nearly matched Aya's.

"Mrs. Du Bois, who is this man?" she demanded, her face red.

"Why Aya," the older belle said, "this wonderful young man is Lunsford."

Taylor smiled and pointed to his face with his thumb. "Well that's what the women call me, but my full name is Taylor Lunsford, the Strapping Space Traveling Aristocrat."

Aya, despite her annoyance with Taylor's first few comments, gave a small bow to him. "Where do you hail from?" she asked politely.

Taylor's eyes illuminated as she did. "Ah, the Aquan way of greeting interstellar travelers," he said in a knowledgeable voice.

Aya's eyes expanded and her mouth hung open wide. "You know about our customs?"

"When you are a brave youthful adventurer, guided by dreams and whims," Taylor responded, his eyes observing her agape expression, "sometimes you venture to places…like Tarabos."

"But…that was so long ago…" Aya responded, murmuring with sadness.

"Aye, it was a beauty but it could be desolate, acrid and full of misery as well," Taylor said, his eyes deep in reflection. "I was fortunate to be traveling with my father before its end."

Aya was silent. Her brain could barely process the words this man said. He was familiar with her planet and she had never met anyone other than Jeeg who shared that knowledge with her.

Seeing the young Aquan freeze in a vacant expression, just gaping at him, Taylor raised his arms. "But I digress, this is a joyous occasion. After all, I did find this young lad lost in the wilderness. And, I found his manly father battling a Noctursa."

"And I would have had that scoundrel lying flat on the ground, if he didn't bust up my arm," Du Bois said, managing a course laugh. "I'm grateful to have a gentleman like you swoop in with your ship and give that monster a good scare."

Jaz's mother clasped her hands to her chest. "I'm forever grateful." Her eyes lit up like they were illuminated by lights. "And, though I haven't asked the hubby yet. I am thinking of having a party at the beer barn in your honor."

Taylor rubbed out a smudge on his helmet and grinned. "I certainly wouldn't mind a toast to me. After all, I've been traveling for several nights without anything but sprouts."

Mr. Du Bois raised his arm and put it around his wife, "Every year my wife has a good idea. And I think the momentous occasion has come for another one." He gazed up at the tall young man who'd rescued him and his son. "I'd love to celebrate this strapping young man, the hero of the day."

"It's settled," Mrs. Du Bois exclaimed, sliding her hands together. "Wives, looks like we have some planning to do." Mrs. Du Bois gave a sly wink at her husband, "And I have a little brown-nosing to do with the hubby so we can plan this party my way."

"Mom, what's brown nosing?" Jaz asked.

Having forgotten her child was there, Du Bois grinned nervously. "Uh, Flora explain this to your brother."

Flora paused for a moment, pondering in her head, before her raising her finger. "It's when you give someone a bag of brown sugar and when they eat from it, they get a little on their nose."

"But what does that have to do with planning a party?" Jaz asked with even more curiosity.

Mrs. Du Bois continued grinning but put her arms on Jaz's shoulders. "Come along dear, you'll understand when you're older."

"Ladies, I humbly accept. It would be rude of me to decline the offer," Taylor said, joining the crowd who left their husbands to gape. "After all, I am the guest of honor."

As the crowd departed and the farmers began to disperse for the forest as well, Flora looked at Aya who stood quietly. She felt she should comfort Aya, but didn't want to earn the ire of her parents again. Knowing this, Aya smiled and waved goodbye to her friend just to let her know she was ok.

Flora nodded and continued on. When everyone was gone, Aya began to converse with her tattoo.

"Child, don't let that smooth talking man-child get to you," Eterna snapped at Aya's uneasy face.

"I didn't," Aya said in proud denial. "It just took me by surprise that he knew about my home. Tarabos never had many visitors from what Jeeg told me."

"That boy, he has an air of familiarity. There's something besides his lecherous nature and bubbling narcissism that I don't like about him. I want you to keep an eye on him," Eterna growled.

"Yes, Eterna," Aya responded. "I want to learn more about him too."

Settling down a little, Eterna spoke in a voice reserved for a doting mother. "But perhaps you can take me to Jeeg. I want to be with my child."

Aya nodded in agreement, stretching her skin to make Eterna smile. She walked back along the outskirts of town to a cabin by the freshwater lake.

The young Aquan and her mentor both loved being close to any body of water; it allowed them to reminisce about their home.

Walking onto the front porch, Aya could see the wood of the cabin glowing white. Unlike the rest of the villages cabin's, Jeeg and Aya had Myron properly honor the Atma tree before cutting it. Like Aya's staff, it shone brightly as a result.

"Nice there are some reverent beings in this insolent village," Eterna spoke to Aya as she opened the door.

Inside the one room cabin, Aya saw Jeeg standing across the room with his back turned. He stood by a small shelf carved in dark wood where he reflected on some heirlooms from his past life.

He held a crimson shell with an upside-down spade like pattern. It was fractured neatly down the middle, but the other half was missing.

Aya quietly shut the door, but as she walked in, Jeeg's ears perked up.

After placing the shell back where it once sat, he turned around and walked to her silently before embracing her in a warm grandfatherly hug.

"Thank the creator," his voice creaked in relief, "I couldn't bear to lose anyone else."

"You're not," Aya told him. "I'm ok. I have a quite a tale to tell you."

Leading Jeeg outside onto the front porch, she spoke of the downed Matriarch Tree, the spiritual upheaval and her encounter with Eterna.

"Can I see her?" Jeeg asked and Aya held her hand out.

"She can move and," Aya said with wide eyes "and she talks to me."

60

Jeeg's hand combed his beard. "Curious, she doesn't move for me."

As Aya puzzled her mind, Eterna spoke up to her. "Child, only you can see can see my spirit move. I am your guide and no one else's."

"Jeeg, so my tattoo, Eterna, she said you won't be able to see her move," Aya said with flushed cheeks. "I'm not making this up I swear!"

"I always believe you," Jeeg responded. "I must be off to check the tree. I need to see the wreckage myself to assess how to help."

Aya looked down at her tattoo and observed the expression Eterna made. She desperately wanted to see her kid and Aya felt it was her duty to alleviate her motherly woes. "Jeeg, where is the Wyrmwolf pup?"

"Ah, so the mother and child wish to be reunited?" Jeeg's wizened eyes looked up at Aya who had already begun to rise. "She's on my bed wrapped in blankets. I wanted the little pup to be cozy."

"Thanks." I hug him with respect. "When things are really important, you're always dependable. I'm sorry for calling you a lazy old man before."

"I was just saving my energy for when it was truly needed," he says with a cheeky grin.

Entering their house again, they walked right to the two Aquan beds. By the window was the pup of silver fur, still fast asleep in Jeeg's bed and tucked in gently. The pup's body was bandaged and dried blood had hardened on the cloth. She breathed out with the soft murmurings of a small mammal.

Aya held her arm and watched the mother release her strife. "I wish I could have said goodbye to my Gardenia," Eterna said with her head bowed.

"You had no choice. You gave it everything you had," Aya responded, feeling the emotion herself.

"Tell Jeeg," the mother said, looking over her child as she rested, "to help raise her to be strong. Please, for this old woman's sake."

Aya did what Eterna commanded, and Jeeg gave a humble bow. "I will consider it my new dharma, oh great elder of the spirit woods." He grabbed his white spirit staff that leaned against the shelf of Aquan heirlooms. "I won't stop there. I'm going to discover what was behind the turmoil in the forest."

Aya turned to face Jeeg as he walked to the door. "Do you need me to do anything?"

"Question anyone who was a witness the night it happened." Jeeg put his hand to his beard. "I heard young Jaz was found. Maybe he will be of some assistance."

"I'll ask him," Aya said with a quick nod.

Jeeg paced out the door and it closed it in a huff.

Aya's face brightened up as she spoke.

"Well done, Eterna. You managed to get Jeeg moving; that's a truly grand feat!" She grabbed her own staff, which leaned against the door. "And I'm going to keep moving too. We will get to the bottom of this in our own way."

"I am truly grateful, Aquan," Eterna responded with a soft and kind voice. "You two are carrying out what I no longer can, and it means the planetoid to me."

Aya stepped outside and surveyed the coast line. Her ears twitched, and she could hear a small, faraway voice coming from the shore. It was Jaz's voice.

"I guess he's playing by the islands again," Aya said. "How could they leave him unattended after what happened? Ugh, he must have run off on his own, ggrhh, again." She growls and exhales sharply.

Aya took off in a sprint towards the coast. Her hands pumping through the air and her breath hot with anger. She didn't understand why Mrs. Du Bois couldn't have anyone look after a child as slippery as this one. Her tune changed when she skidded to a stop and saw Jaz with his hands curled up into a makeshift telescope. "Well, Jaz Island will be a go today," he said to himself like a young adventurer.

"Jaz what are you doing here all alone?" Aya questioned in a very concerned voice.

"I'm not all alone, Aya." Jaz responded earnestly.

A loud release of air came from above Aya, spooking her and causing her to wobble backwards. She quickly regained balance and draw her staff into defensive position.

Aya looked up and felt the heat of exhaust as a spaceship the size of her cabin's roof landed next to her. It was purple and blue lined, cylindrical with glider wings built for speedy sleekness in the outer rims of space. Its dark windows formed a small dome that protected the passengers of the spaceship. The only thing Aya could see on it was an emblazoned decal of a bolt of white lightning with the shapely legs of an adult humanoid female crossed in a cheesecake pose.

"Jaz, get back!" Aya screamed and whacked the purple and blue lined cylindrical ship repeatedly.

"Hey Aquan, ease up on my ship," a familiar voice snapped. "She's been through hell already."

The dark glass over the cockpit slid back revealing Taylor's conceited mug.

Aya walked around to the cone shaped nose of the vehicle to see that it was badly crunched inward. "What happened to this vehicle?" Aya asked with sudden suspicion.

Taylor hopped down between Jaz and Aya. His long hair following him down in a graceful manner.

"Whoa, he's so cool!" Jaz yelled.

"You ever piloted through an asteroid field, Aquan?" Taylor asked with a chill demeanor.

"My name is Aya. And I have only flown through space once." Aya shirked her presence over a touched nerve. "I will never do it again."

"Then you never want to go through an asteroid field. Dinged my woman up real good," Taylor responded. "And you know what they say, an unhappy wife means an unhappy life."

Eterna growled. "He treats objects as women and women as objects. I know his silver-tongued kin all too well."

Aya looked up from her arm and gave a tough glare at Taylor to let him know she meant business. "Taylor, why are you here and what are you doing with Jaz?"

Taylor remained unphased by the hostile glance of a warrior. Instead, he gave a little chuckle. "I like you, Aya, though you do seem a little tight assed and you keep talking to yourself. Your quirks just make you…unique."

He strolled over to Aya, moving into her personal bubble and causing her to leap to a defensive stance with a reddened face. "If you want to know why I'm here. The farm ladies wanted to keep their little party under wraps so I'm watching the young spud for them."

"He's not watching me. We're partners in crime," Jaz said with a wide grin. "He's going to fly me to Jaz Island so I can claim it. Oh, and he's gonna give me tips for gettin' the chicks."

"Let's focus on one thing at a time," Taylor said with a confident smirk to match it. "And remember kiddo, you can't name that beauty 'til you claim her."

"I've already called dibs on it so it's mine. Right, big brother?" Jaz asked with a toothy grin as Taylor hoisted him into his purple space cruiser.

Aya gritted her teeth over his words. She was never called "big sister" by Jaz despite all they've been through.

Aya tried to shrug it off as a mere annoyance, but it lingered with her causing Taylor and Eterna to both call her name as she stared into space.

Taylor laughed. "Seems I'm not the only space cadet. We have more in common by the second. Aya, Listen…" He walked closer to Aya again and leaned up against his spaceship.

His eyes met hers with a peculiar glance; it was both self-satisfied but also interested in her.

"Don't be so serious. Life's a garden of misfortune and delight. Just gotta know which trees to pick from."

Taylor leaped onto the wing of his space cruiser and then jumped into the cockpit. He gave the befuddled Aquan a playful salute. "With these words of wisdom I have graciously imparted upon you, I hope you learn to live a little, Aya. Because if you don't, who else will? Farewell, my sweet Aquan."

The cockpit closed around Taylor and Jaz and the ship hovered before zooming all the way to the levitating islands over the lake.

"I wish that man's tongue had been severed from his maw," Eterna chimed in as Aya stood still with an expression of confusion.

"We have no idea what Jaz saw. And now he's out of reach." Aya shook her head. "Aya, why are you just standing there?"

"That man…" Aya said with a look of intrigue. "I don't know why, but I want to learn more about him. His eyes, they perplex me, and I don't like the effect he has over Jaz."

"He is like slime in a swamp, covers all he can reach with his self-righteous muck," Eterna responded with disdain. "There's always parasites looking to cling onto those with power. Better to remain without a mate than to pair with a leech."

"He's very different from the men who've flirted with me in the village," Aya added, her eyes revealing a passionate curiosity. "They were stupid and driven purely by impulse. He isn't letting on who he truly is or his honest intent. It's…distracting," she says with a light blush.

"That I agree with absolutely," Eterna said with a nod. "He's dangerous and untrustworthy…"

"I don't trust him…either," Aya quietly agreed as Allons ran to the shore.

"Miss Aya," he said, out of breath. "Jeeg requires you. It's about that dern spirit tree. He found something at it."

"Great," Eterna said, "we can at least advance on that front. Aya get yourself together, we're going to solve this."

Aya gazed out to the sea one last time. She thought of the words Taylor had first spoken to her of her lost planet. "Aye, it was a beauty but it could be desolate, acrid and full of misery as well."

He was referring to the opposite side of Tarabos when he called it desolate. It was a desert area very few Aquans ever ventured into because of the hostile climates, black dream chimer snakes and dangerous sand sharks.

Just who was he? And why was he so knowledgeable of her planet? It was just a memory kept alive by her and Jeeg.

Aya finally pulled herself away and headed off towards the spirit forest. She knew her sworn duty called for her to be present in the here and now, but now her mind was pre-occupied with the growing mystery of the traveler Taylor Lunsford.

THE HOWLING HAUNTS

Chapter 6

Aya sped across the grassy seaside field, staff in hand. The wind blew past her as Eterna spoke to the young Aquan warrior. "Child, I know that nasty man has got you confused and hormonal. It's all part of youth. I felt the same when I was your age."

"I'm not hormonal," Aya snapped loudly at her tattoo. "This has nothing to do with hormones. He knows about my past world."

"So, this is what your strange behavior is about?" Eterna responded frankly. "You sure it's not because you see him as a potential mate?"

Aya grinded to a stop. "Eterna, no offense, but you seem to be taking his words and actions more personally than me." The tattoo of the elder Wyrmwolf was silent so Aya continued. "Do you have some kind of personal vendetta against him?"

The tattoo cast her eye aside from Aya's curious glance, before muttering. "I had a mate like Lunsford. Him and I begat Gardenia and though I would never speak ill of him in front of our child, I loathed him and everything he stood for."

Aya's bright blue eyes widened. She clutched her arm band, sliding it up to reveal more of Eterna. "Tell me about him. I need advice, okay?"

"I know we don't have much time. I'll give you the abridged tome of my follies," Eterna said. "When my father bestowed me with the power of the guardian, he didn't consider the consequences of making a female Wyrmwolf the matriarch."

68

"Which was?" Aya asked, her eyes intently focused on Eterna's inky maw.

"When I met my mate," Eterna continued, "he was as smooth and polished as a rock lizard's scales. Always very flirtatious and briming with magnetism and charisma. His slick demeanor never letting on to what he truly craved...power."

Eterna closed her eyes and gave a soft pause. "We mated and when we had a child, he showed his true colors. 'Now that you're a mother, you'll have other duties. I think it's best you let an alpha male like me lead our kind'."

The Wyrmwolf tattoo opened her eyes and gave Aya an emotionally pained, but angry glare. "I bared my teeth and told him 'I will never step down and shirk the responsibility my father bestowed upon me.'"

Eterna snarled and flashed her sharp teeth like she would tear Aya's skin and break free. "He continued with his insistence, at first gently but soon, rabidly, pressing me further and further. He snarled at me like he would sink his teeth into me at any second."

Aya placed her hand on her wolf tattoo to offer comfort.

Eterna's voice grew higher and more distressed as she continued her story. "Howling back, I responded, 'If that's all you loved me for, I never want you in the presence of me or my child again. Leave me!'"

Aya watched as her spirit guide companion's head sunk down solemnly. "After that night, I never saw him again. Disloyal scoundrel, I hope another Wyrmwolf crunched his face off."

Aya ran her fingers across the tattoo of the great Wyrmwolf. "Surely you don't mean that."

Eterna looked up with shock on her face. "You are such a gentle spirit for an Aquan child. But don't be naïve, men will try twice as hard to dethrone a woman in power. Just because they think it'll be easy."

Aya responded softly. "You're contradicting yourself." She sighs. "Look, I've never had a relationship before, but I felt your pain when you spoke of your betrayal. I don't know if I'd ever wish death on someone who scorned me though. I don't think I want that energy in me."

"You don't have to harbor hate, Aquan. Just be wary of this man," Eterna responded, her voice becoming very motherly and protective like Aya was her own pup. "Don't confide in him about yourself. Don't show any weakness to him. You'll never know his true intentions, until it's too late."

Aya picked up her feet and began running again. Atma trees hung in the distance, and so did a crowd of farmers. "Don't worry, Eterna. The safety of this planetoid is my absolute priority."

"Thank you, child," Eterna said, finally showing a smile. "I entrusted the right being with the powers of the guardian."

Aya found herself in the midst of a crowd who were standing on the outskirts of the forest.

Farmers were scowling and grumbling, and Aya ran to them to address their concerns. Upon closer observation, many of the men looked fearful and full of trepidation. She located Myron with his small spectacled face. "What's happened? Why are you all standing here?"

"The woods are haunted and dark. We can't even dust the trees anymore," he said solemnly.

"Look what happened to Gully," another cried.

Two farmers propped up a man known for his blotchy red face. He was pale and shivering and his legs were limp.

Aya crouched on her legs and examined Gully as he stuttered out his breaths. It was the first time she ever felt sorry for a man who had chastised her and her ways.

She looked to Eterna who used her knowledgeable existence to her advantage. "He is suffering from spectral shock. The spirits can do that to a mortal; but don't worry, as long as he eats a dose of soul fruit, he'll feel a lot better."

"I somehow shook that off while climbing the mountain," Aya said to Eterna.

"Shook what off?" asked the bearded man holding Gully.

"Uh, spectral shock. Those ghosts inflicted the same thing upon Gully."

The bearded man raised an eyebrow, "And…how do you know these things?"

Aya rose to her feet and got close to the bearded man's face. "Don't you see the way I dress? I'm pretty damn spiritual," she said with a sassy purse of her lips before looking back at Gully in his condition. "We need to get him some soul fruit. It will help him recover."

Allons ran panting to the group. He collapsed onto the ground and sat in a cross-legged position. "Miss Aya, you run so fast, there's no way I could catch up with you."

"Was there something else you wanted to tell me, Allons?" Aya asked, looking down at him.

"Yeah…Jeeg," Allons said panting, slowly lowering his back to the soft verdant grass "he found the cause of these ghosts."

Aya walked through the crowd who all gaped at her wide eyed.

"Is she really going in there?" they whispered as she walked into the spirit woods.

She looked up and saw the Atma trees had changed color and spread their leaves differently. They had shed their rainbow sheen and became tarp-like, extending their reach across acres of land.

Darkness draped over the woods and Aya could barely see the horizon. A musky scent hung over the forest as grass and small plants shriveled from lack of sunlight. Nothing seemed to thrive in the forest anymore.

"Eterna," Aya asked while she shivered, "what has become of the spirit woods?"

"I can't be certain," the Wyrmwolf guide responded, "but it seems the forest is extracting revenge on those who wronged it."

Aya thought of what Jeeg had instructed her about her religion. "We are all part of the big dream," she muttered under her breath.

"Careful child," Eterna spoke aloud. "I sense the spectral presence has grown since the night. Ghosts of ancient beasts roam these parts."

Aya nodded and pressed forward. She clutched her staff tightly and focused all of her own spiritual energy into its soulful white bark.

The staff illuminated allowing Aya to see a few feet in front of her, but just barely.

Aya could feel the normally warm air occasionally disturbed by a chilling wind that made the wispy hair on her neck stand up. The forest once rife with chirps, barks and grunts sat still in a desolate silence, making what lied in the darkness all the more concealed and ominous.

The Aquan jerked her head around when she heard the sound of a Wyrmwolf.

It wasn't a normal growl, it sounded more like a deep moan. She drew more breath as the air around her grew stale and frigid. She could feel the rustle of cold, rough fur against her back but when she spun around again, there was nothing tangible. Her normally tall stature shrank, and Eterna spoke again.

"Do not fear the specters, child. Though their presence has grown, their business remains tied to this planetoid."

"I won't," Aya said in return, "but I can feel their anguish. It freezes everything with sadness."

As she spoke, Aya heard a voice unlike the guttural moan. It was a small whine, a cry similar to a lost child in the middle of a deep, dark forest. It came from the distance and Aya lowered her staff like a flashlight in order to see farther. She could see a small body shining bright green. She ran to it, ignoring any caution she previously had.

Upon closer expectation, the glowing body belonged to a tiny Wyrmwolf pup.

Aya quickly called out in the dry air. "What troubles you, little spirit?"

The pup with hollow black pupils looked directly into Aya's soul with its glare. He whined again and Eterna spoke, "He says 'He was playing in the forest. Along with some friends. The sky grew dark. My friends fled. I don't know why. Where did they go?"

The pup's eyes though hollow seemed to grow deeper as it whined further. It pained Aya's ears to hear such a shrill, otherworldly cry.

Eterna continued on, "I heard strange footsteps. Then hand held me down. Something sharp…it hurt so much. I…" Eterna gasped before speaking again. "I never saw another year."

The pups whining grew more intense and rang out through the forest.

Aya felt she could hear multiple cries as well; and then, the pup fell over, revealing an enormous knife wound before dissolving into spectral dust.

Aya spoke softly. "This must have happened before we came and changed Du Bois' mind."

Eterna with a look of grief cried. "Humans! Only those monsters would do this to a child."

Aya's head swayed as she closed her eyes. "They're not all like that. Flora has never harmed an animal. In fact, Wyrmwolves have done more harm to her."

Eterna howled from Aya's arm, causing her arm to writhe. "I would never forgive them if they brought harm to my pup."

"You have my word," Aya said, massaging her arm. "I will continue to bring balance so nothing like that happens again."

"Bless you, Aya," Eterna said softly through her raspy tear-soaked voice.

Aya pressed on, heading further and further into the heart of the woods. She heard cries from all around her and it made her heart sick. She saw another light in the distance and ran to it.

She found Jeeg standing with his staff glowing by the ruins of the downed Matriarch tree. Pale green fog swirled around the blackened remains. It glowed sickly.

"There you are," he said. "I'm glad you've found your way to me. It is truly ghastly around here."

"Do you know what's happening?"

"Yes." Jeeg extended his hand into the light of his staff. "I believe the spirits of downed Wyrmwolves and other beasts were residing within the Matriarch tree. It kept them at peace for centuries; but now, the tree has been laid waste."

"Is that correct Eterna?" Aya looked down at her tattoo. "That's correct," Eterna said and Aya relayed that message to Jeeg.

"Can we channel the spirits in any way?" Aya asked. "I mean we do have staffs made of spirit wood."

Jeeg shook his head. "It'd take a staff the size of the Matriarch to placate all of these enraged spirits. You have other responsibilities now." He reached into his robe's side pocket and removed a small piece of spirit fruit. "I'm going to attempt to raise another tree."

"But won't that take centuries?"

Jeeg faced Aya and placed a robed hand on her shoulder. He looked into her frantic eyes with his calm and wizened ones. "When you're young, your patience is fleeting. But when you reach my age, you'll have learned the greatest things take several lifetimes to grow. Your children's children will rest under a new matriarch tree like you once did when you were young."

Aya's nodded with a soothed look on her face. "I understand. "Do you know how it fell?"

Jeeg raised his wrinkled fingers to his long goatee. "That my young Aya, has puzzled me. I know how it happened, but it is still unbelievable."

Aya's eyes shimmered in her staff's light. "How?"

"It was struck by lightning." Jeeg reached down and picked up a piece of splintered wood. "The way the wood is split would shows a lightning strike was the cause, but the way the tree fell, and the marks of the surrounding foliage, indicate it came at a horizontal angle."

Jeeg turned to Aya holding the wood. "This was not an act of nature."

Aya held her hands to her mouth. "This is no time for levity, Jeeg. Do you think it was a projectile?"

"It could very much be, but no one on this planet has that kind of weaponry," Jeeg responded duly to his friend.

Eterna growled. "What about that rake's ship?"

"Did it have weaponry?" Aya asked. "I didn't look close enough at it."

"That womanizer destroyed the matriarch tree," Eterna said with a newfound drive in her eyes. "His crime against nature won't go unpunished."

Aya put her hand to her mouth to hastily bite a longer fingernail clean. "He's tricky like a fox. I don't think after the good he has done for the villagers, that they will believe he is the one responsible. I'll have to find evidence and corner him to come clean."

"We just have to catch him in a lie," Eterna retorted. "This party that the human mother spoke of is the perfect opportunity to do so."

"Ah, the party," Aya said as her eyes lit up. "Good thinking, wolf momma!" She taps her tattoo with a grin, the tattoo grimaces back.

Jeeg stood around confused. "What party do you speak of?"

"Mrs. Du Bois' party at the beer barn. She's throwing one in honor of Taylor finding Jaz."

The old man's snow-white eyebrows raised. "That sounds like a good occasion for us to bring our instruments. We can play something to lament over the forest's loss, and hopefully soothe the spirits so they don't enter the village." Jeeg pointed his finger forward and with a sheepish grin asked, "Have you been practicing Aya?"

Aya took a step back. Aya's face tensed up and she began to whine and plead. "All the craziness in town has distracted me from frivolous hobbies."

"That excuse is only valid for one day," Jeeg said, giving a raspy chuckle. "But I'll let it slide. I know you're an Aquan who loves running through the fields rather than sitting around playing the old Luta-Flute."

Aya let out a sigh of relief. "Thanks, I hoped you'd understand. Let's get back and maybe I'll go through my scales a bit."

Jeeg nodded and the two held their staffs out to their sides. With the combined power of two illuminated spirit wood staffs, the tense spirts stayed away from the Aquans but watched them from a safe distance while moaning still, their cries reminding Jeeg, Aya and Eterna of their mission.

REVELATIONS & REVELRY

Chapter 7

The beer barn was a former two-story barn that housed fruits in the first floor and condensed them down to liquids on the second floor. It had become a regular hot spot for farmers who wanted to drink liquids from fermented fruit. Eventually Mrs. Du Bois, who changed the upper floor that was already full of handmade juicers into a place to serve thirsty customers. It was a popular place for town meetings and parties, including the one held on this very day.

Though the tension was thick over the changes within the spirit woods, the juices and merriment lifted the villager's spirits. Only Jeeg and Aya remained wary of the future.

Jeeg hoped this night would bring the wrongdoer to justice. He elected not to tell the villagers the full extent of the forest's problems until things settled down and the culprit was subdued.

Jeeg and Aya were perched on a small raised area in back of the beer barn as they entertained the villagers at the night party.

Jeeg strummed a large wooden triple necked zitar with sixteen strings. The instrument covered every octave in the Tarabosian key, a key previously unknown to humans. The key was normally inaudible to humans who didn't sport the long, pointed ears of Tarabos natives; and until it could be tuned down on their instruments, humans never heard it. Many first-time listeners were captivated by the unusual, but spirit lifting tones.

Jeeg's long fingers picked at his instrument with spindle like precision. They moved slowly but never missed a single note.

Aya, in contrast, hastily panted into a wooden flute with three different ends. It was trident shaped and each end was separated by an adjustable gate. When all gates were open, they could reach the Tarabosian octave.

Aya had to keep a frantic pace to make sure she hit all the notes perfectly, but she knew she wasn't cut out for the job. She wasn't a natural born musician; she took it upon herself to keep every facet of her culture alive.

The music Jeeg and Aya played together didn't have a name, but the townsfolk called it folk-blues-mysticism. True to the blues, the lyrics Jeeg sung in his scratchy, aged voice betrayed his experiences:

I hold your hand, strolling through silver sands that shine on this island

We sail through shining seas, catching sparkling shells and each other's glance

The hazy air as you laugh seems so unreal

I reach for your hand again, but your touch I can no longer feel

I awake, turning inside and out, it was just a dream

A dream and nothing more, my mind's hollow scheme

When I finally walk beside your smiling face

I'll realize, I've died and gone to a celestial place

Only Flora Du Bois sat by them. She was on a stool with her legs crossed and her long flowing white dress draped over it. When the song came to an end, she clapped excitedly. "Oh yay, please do another one Mr. Jeeg. I do love tales of unrequited love."

Jeeg pretended to survey his audience. Everyone else was drinking and standing around Du Bois who was touting the feats of Taylor. "Does the audience have any other requests?" He winked to Aya who had tired from blowing into her flute.

Jeeg gave a bitter laugh. "To think in the first year we came to this planet, they said my music was otherworldly, heartrending and mystical. Now it's the background din at a party."

"Hey, it takes the heat off my bad performance," said Aya with a mischievous grin.

"Back to work, lackey," Jeeg responded while wagging his finger, "We have another tale of unrequited love coming right up."

Aya gave another reluctant puff into her Luta-Flute when familiar boots of leather stood in front of her. "This music is such a downer. We're supposed to be having a party."

She looked up to see Taylor's self-satisfied face, now sporting a trademark uniform worn by male members of the Du Bois family. He was clad in a light dress shirt with dark suspenders that contrasted with his tanned skin and hair. It made him look dashing even if they were clothes that belong to Du Bois. He lightly ran his hand through the hair covering his ear, and slid up his white cuff-link.

Aya glared at him for his disrespectful comment. "And what kind of music are we supposed to play at a party?"

"That is the question, Aya, and I am the keeper of the answer." Taylor slid out a small device.

It was flat and dark with a screen that illuminated when he touched it.

Aya was bewildered by the bright lights and colors that flashed on a device as flat as a flapjack.

"Ah, here it is," Taylor smiled as loud flashy sounds blared from the device.

The device blared colorful noise with rhythmic yet mechanical sounding drums and vocals that sounded encoded and robotic. It echoed around the beer barn.

Aya crossed her arms in disproval and grimaced. "Would you really trust a machine to make music that should come from the heart?"

Taylor looked Aya over as he typically did before grinning. "If you don't like it, why are you shaking that booty?"

Aya looked down at her body. It was rhythmically shaking and her foot was tapping. She felt like dancing even if her mind felt scorn. "It's nothing, just a butt spasm. The creator would never accept this kind of music."

"I dunno," Taylor said with a raise of his voice. "Everyone loves to get funky. Even Aquans who play music fit for a funeral."

Jeeg frowned at the young man as his hands rested on his zitar. "This is music of my long lamentable past."

"Why moan about the past, old man?" Taylor asked. "All we have is right now. Enjoy it before we fade away."

Jeeg looked at the floor, eyeing Taylor up from his leather boots to the top of his conditioned hair. He rose from his chair, placing his zitar on it and extended a hand forward. "You're right. Care to dance?"

Taylor begrudgingly looked at the old man who was heading towards him, before letting out a sigh. "I may as well humor you because you're not going to be around much longer."

Jeeg grasped Taylor's hands, taking him by surprise. "We're going to do this my way," he responded before hollering. "Aya, the Aquatic Waltz."

Aya began to play a swaying but bubbly tune on her Luta-flute, setting the stage for Jeeg and Taylor who slid back and forth on the dance floor.

Flora watched with her head resting on her hands as she grinned.

Bubbles began to rise from the alcoholic drinks of the villagers as they all turned to watch the very first showing of the Aquatic Waltz.

"Your grip is tenacious old man," Taylor sneered.

"The last one I gripped like that, loved me until the very end," the old man responded.

Aya glanced and smiled at Taylor and Jeeg as she played her Luta-flute. They moved as one, and it was surprising to see a rakish man like Taylor devoting time to entertaining the elderly Jeeg. She was even more surprised that he knew exactly how to move to this otherwise forgotten tune of the Aquan race. Her interest in his worldliness grew as her eyes watched them swaying back and forth.

The crowd of villagers gathered around the two and watched mesmerized. When the music finally stopped, there was an applause from everyone, even Mr. Du Bois.

Jeeg walked back to where Aya was, his face was beaming.

"How was it?" Aya asked Jeeg as he lifted his robe onto the small stage.

"I'm pleasantly surprised by that spaceman's dancing abilities," Jeeg said, his eyes losing their forlorn sheen. "It transported me back to our own planet…just for a few minutes."

"And how was my playing?"

"Surprisingly in tune."

Aya looked to Taylor who was receiving accolades for his abilities with a bow.

Had he danced with Aquans before? Her curiosity thickened, when suddenly he approached her.

"May I have this dance?" He asked in a voice that was oh-so-suave.

Aya looked from side to side, before pointing to herself wordlessly.

Taylor smiled. "Yes, you."

Jeeg patted Aya on the back. "Go, he has already proved his worth as a dancer."

Aya slowly reached out her hand as if about to dip her hand in ice cold water.

Taylor, seeing her momentarily inching forward, capitalized on the moment and led her to the center of the dance floor.

"W-w-what kind of dance do you want to do?" Aya stuttered.

"The kind of dance you do with a beautiful young woman. One that's nice and slow." He took one of Aya's hands in his and placed his other softly on her hip.

Jeeg began to strum an old Tarabosian melody, an ode to the elven lovers of legend who formed the land and sea on Tarabos. The two began to move slowly together.

Aya's heart thumped like she had undergone a vigorous dash across the plains of the planetoid. She had never danced with a young man before. None of the villagers ever caught her fancy, but as she looked into Taylor's eyes, which were dreamier and fuller than his words, she felt overcome by a fluttery sensation.

Suddenly, she felt bashful. Her prideful feelings became quite the opposite and it led her to avert her face.

"Why'd you look away?" Taylor asked, dropping his smooth visage for a second.

"I don't know," Aya muttered quietly. "I've looked a Noctursa dead in the eye before. I don't know what's the problem with you."

"Are you saying I look like a bear?"

Aya shook her head. "No, no, not at all. You're not fuzzy." She began to nervously laugh, but Taylor looked into her eyes again and she looked up again.

"You look beautiful. All the flora and fauna of this world can't compare," he said.

"You haven't seen the light garden under the moonlight."

"Oh, is that an invitation?"

Aya lit up.

Taylor lifted her chin and gave her a calming smile. "Let's just enjoy this moment together."

Taylor moved his hands to Aya's sides, gripping slightly around her rear and Aya attempted to follow suit on Taylor's sides.

"No, these go on my shoulders," he smiled gallantly.

Aya quickly moved them to his shoulders, and she finally felt comfortable in this position. The two swayed together back and forth as Jeeg picked the strings in a way that imitated the hearts of lovers. For a moment, Aya quickly forgot every suspicion Eterna had instilled in her. She forgot everyone else was there too. Her tough demeanor gave way to her childhood dreams of living as royalty in the sea castle of the king of the Aquans, engaged to a noble prince. It was a childlike whim, but she occasionally indulged it while she lay asleep in her bed.

"Hey, Miss Aquan," Taylor said, snapping his fingers "the dance is over."

Jeeg had picked his final cadences and everyone stood around applauding.

Du Bois, the victim of more than a few beverages of fermented fruit caused Aya to snap back into reality. He stood up with his good arm raised.

"I thought old men was an odd choice, but this gentleman will even dance with earians. Is there nothing he won't do?"

Aya chuckled to herself. Was he so drunk that he forgot about Jeeg's lineage? Such a foolish hateful man.

"Sorry, good sir, but there are a few ladies waiting for a dance. You'll have to wait your turn." Taylor flicked his hair as the villagers clamored for more.

"Haha! And he's got wit!" Du Bois raised his arm again. His face bright red and stance wobbly. "Say it with him, folks."

With Taylor's assistance the crowd began to chant. "Taylor Lunsford, The Strapping Space Traveling Aristocrat."

Mr. Du Bois tried to follow along, but instead said, "the Traveling Space Strapping Aristostrap" and wobbled into Taylor.

"Whoa there," Taylor responded putting his arm around the drunken man. "You might want to take it easy, Mr. Du Bois."

Another farmer pulled up a seat and allowed Du Bois to sit. "I'll take it easy," he guffawed, "when you tell everyone how you saved me and my son with a sky ship. You're a hero."

"Well, well…if you insist," Taylor said, trying to calm the terribly plastered man. "I happened to be in your area when I was seeking refuge during my deep space interstellar travel journey. I was scouring the spirit forest in search of any sign of intelligent life to help refresh me. That's when I stumbled across a strange happening."

Eterna called to Aya, "Listen carefully, child. I want you to pick out holes in this man's tale so we can confront him."

Aya smiled with a light whisper, "I will. Also, I'm surprised you didn't berate me during the dance."

"It's fine to have fun just as long you remove your head from the clouds when needed."

Taylor struck a pose. "I was flying by a mountain and this boy landed right on my windshield." Taylor held his hands out in front of his face. "A true space pilot is used to all kinds of debris breezing by his window, but nothing alive. It was truly outstanding. I quickly landed, and found that he was unconscious with a minor head trauma."

"Jaz…" Aya murmured "he was unconscious."

"I guess that human child's account is no good," Eterna replied.

Not hearing Aya, Taylor continued on. "I heard cries in the forest rain and I hovered slowly above, surveying the land, until I saw bold Mr. Du Bois battling for his life against a ravenous Noctursa. The beast slashed his arm and he fell backwards. Witnessing the attack, I stood atop my spaceship and leapt down! That's when I…" Taylor bent down, and drew something from his pocket: a bright red dagger made out of metal intertwined with red electricity "I scared that beast off with a flash of my dagger and my ship's bright lights."

Everyone cheered and housewives much older than him swooned. Du Bois exclaimed, "That sounds so exciting. I wish I was there!"

"You were there," Mrs. Du Bois said, frowning.

"That beast had knocked my lights out faster than a couple shots did," Du Bois responded, pointing into open space.

Eterna called loudly to Aya. "I didn't tell you this, but the last things I saw before I was attacked and was blinded was a blinding flash of white and red."

Aya quickly pulled her inked companion up to her face. Her eyes were wide with concern. "Do you think he used a similar attack on you?"

Eterna gave an affirmative nod. "This is certainly not a coincidence. Let's find an opportunity to discover more."

Aya stood up from her chair after a moment's thought. "I'm going to confront him alone outside."

Eterna's looked at Aya with shock. "He's dangerous and…"

"Eterna, I'm just going to ask him a few questions," Aya said. "Perhaps this was a misunderstanding, but if not, I can take him. I've subdued much bigger beasts than a lying man with a dull dagger."

"It's not his size that's dangerous," Eterna responded, "it's his mind. Child, I hope you know what you're doing."

Aya bobbed her head forward. "I do."

As Aya approached Taylor, he was shrugging off marriage proposals.

Du Bois had slumped to his knees from where he sat and was looking up at Taylor. "Please lord, please take my eldest daughter Flora's hand in marriage. Please, so she doesn't have to wed my brother's son."

Flora held her hands to her face. "Oh father, don't ask him that. It's so embarrassing."

"I promise eleven toes are her only physical defect," Du Bois cried out, as his wife tried to drag him away and soothe him.

Flora ran off too, her face as bright red as her father's, despite not drinking a drop of alcohol.

"Taylor," Aya said with a gruff voice, trying to call to him amidst the circus.

The man, in response, narrowed his eyes in a look of defensive skepticism. "What's up? You look like you want to fight me, Aya."

Aya quickly realized she was making Taylor apprehensive. Instead, she tried her hardest to sound like Flora. She raised her voice to a sweet, lilting pitch and tilted her head. She put her hand on her hip; and even

88

though it was awkward with such a tall body, she hoped she still possessed some feminine wiles.

"I want to talk to you outside…er about mystical things and nature," she said brushing her hand through her short fluffy bob and rolling her head along with it.

Taylor raised his eyebrows and released a small puff of air. In his naturally deep voice, he spoke "I'd love to learn about your nature, Miss Aquan."

He avoided the sharp glares of the housewives and their spotty daughters and followed Aya out of the beer barn into the night.

They exited down the creaky wooden staircase that led to the bar portion of the beer barn, and strolled through the village.

Taylor was unusually silent, and it made Aya more wary.

They strolled past the village, past Jeeg and Aya's house and off to the sea swept coast where sea birds whistled in the night. The sky was open like a grand theater. It was alight with many stars and far out planetoids. It made Aya think of her home before anything else.

"So why have you brought me here, mystery girl?" Taylor asked in a deep voice.

"Well, first," Aya said, her normally abrasive tone altering itself to a friendlier one, "I wanted to say thanks."

Taylor looked confused for his first time in front of her. "Thanks…? For?"

"For dancing with Jeeg," Aya said with her hands behind her back. "He may not look like it, but he's been depressed for a very long time."

"I can tell. Good musicians don't lie about their feelings," Taylor said. "They're like dogs who howl in the night with pure unadulterated emotion."

"Oh. I never thought of it like that before," Aya said, before a pause and she spoke in a candid voice. "Taylor, I wanted to ask you something,"

"Oh really? About what? I am quite an opinionated man so I'll most certainly have an answer for you."

Aya looked at her tattoo. She observed Eterna urging her to ask about any harm he brought to the planetoid. She put her aside and looked up at Taylor's dark eyes. Her mind grew flustered, and she started to wonder who this man was.

Was he malevolent like Eterna felt or was he a good man like the villagers believed?

"So…uh how was life for you on Tarabos?" Aya blurted out.

"Child, what on this holy planetoid are you doing?" Eterna snapped at Aya.

Aya ignored her and stuffed her hand into her pant pocket.

"What did you say?" Taylor asked, his eyes widening.

"Tarabos?" Aya choked out. "How was life on Tarabos?"

"Like I said, I just visited for a short time," Taylor said, nonchalantly. "Saw some sights and I left. My father and I were nothing more than tourists."

Aya couldn't believe what she was hearing. She could tell he was playing it off now, but why and what for? She continued to press him even while Eterna continued to yap at her. "But what about it being desolate and full of misery like you said?"

"Isn't that true of most planets?" Taylor responded with a lift of his hands and a shrug of his shoulders. "But within the misery, you can always unearth a gem." He grasps her hands.

Aya bared her fangs. She finally had Taylor alone and could ask him about her world, but he playing games.

Taylor through gazing at the angry Aquan could sense that her friendliness and patience were starting to unravel. "Look, Missy, you can drop the girlish demeanor," Taylor replied. "We both know that's not true to who you are. But I don't know what you want from me."

Aya thrusted a finger into Taylor's face. "I want you to stop toying with me." She turned away and her voice began to quiver. "You don't know how it feels to lose your whole world and live in a place where only one other soul knows it existed."

"I'm sorry. I just happen to have a very selective memory and I don't remember anything specific about your world," Taylor responded with another shoulder shrug.

He began to walk away, but Aya turned to him and yelled. "You are nothing but a fraud. Someone who lies and deceives people just for your own amusement. A lying, no-good serpent."

Aya had called upon imagery of the townspeople who believed that the root of all evil was a mythical snake.

Taylor turned around and his demeanor visibly changed. For the first time, he looked hurt and angered.

Aya wasn't sure what words set him off, but he began to stomp towards her.

The Aquan continued. "You may have deceived this village, but I know you were the one who destroyed the Matriarch tree."

"You don't know anything about me." Taylor drew his electrified red dagger and swung it into Aya's spirit wood staff. "I destroyed that tree by accident. I hit it when I aimed to shoot the bear that attacked Du Bois. But now that I've seen what it's done to your planetoid, I can't let you tell anyone."

Aya panted as she held her staff tightly. She felt her chest thump from the adrenaline as she sensed Taylor's bloodlust boil. "You could have come clean, but instead you used your mistake to be worshipped as a hero. You disgust me."

Taylor swung again, and Aya pirouetted quickly whacking him on the back of his thigh. He bent over in agony. "You think it's easy to do the right thing in a tricky situation," he growled. "You clearly haven't been in a lot of tricky situations yourself."

"My whole planet was destroyed!" Aya screamed as she avoided a crouched attempt at stabbing her.

She furiously whacked Taylor on the back of the head, causing his head to jerk forward. He leaned forward spitting blood.

"Okay," he gasped, his voice raspy from sudden blood in his throat. "I'll come clean."

Aya put her staff to her side. "Good…" she said, before Taylor leaped up and stabbed her in the stomach with his knife.

She let out a choke as she felt both electricity and metal course through her body.

"Aya," Eterna cried out as she fell to the ground and her staff fell aside.

Her thoughts began to flash in her head. She expected her life to roll past her eyes, but instead she saw a white Wyrmwolf born among other pups. She saw the Wyrmwolf bitten by a much larger greying Wyrmwolf and felt the power transform the Wyrmwolf into something greater.

Aya felt a fierce wild impulse and she crawled to her feet. She began to feel her fingernails sharpen, her ears retreated to the top of her head and her face extend into a snout. Her body hunched over and grew into a different form-the form of a canine. She let out a howl as wings expanded from her back.

She had transformed into a silver Wyrmwolf. She was the spitting image of Eterna and the only thing that marked Aya's identity was her long brown earrings still hanging from her wolf incarnation's ears.

She wobbled a little, unused to moving on four feet.

Seeing Taylor had fallen back in shock, she sprang onto him. Snarling and growling, she poised herself to tear his throat out. Her sharp maw dripped as it thirsted for his demise.

Taylor's knife had fallen from his hands, flying across the sand to where he couldn't reach it and Aya could tell he was ready to submit to death.

The cry of townsfolk shook both the wild Aquan and the terrified human.

Aya could see that a large group of humans were coming through her vision. Worried how they would react to her presence, she ran off.

She turned around to growl loudly at Taylor as he reached onto his shirt and realized she had torn the front, leaving his chest exposed.

Aya shuffled off into the forest as fast as she could. She had no idea what had caused these circumstances behind her transformation, but there were two things she knew at the moment: she had to find a way to become an Aquan again and warn everyone about the despicable fraud, Taylor Lunsford.

OLD WING & NEW LIFE

Chapter 8

Aya was carried by pure motivation, practically flying to her destination alone. As soon as she reached the vestiges of the now darkened spirit wood, her legs became tangled and she fell flat on the ground.

She had no idea how to walk as a quadruped.

She let out a loud howl in frustration. It echoed through the trees that stood withering in the silent night. She tried to call out for Eterna's guidance, but she was no longer in commune with the great Wyrmwolf spirit.

She was alone for her first time as a guardian.

For a long while, she sat pondering her fate. She realized that Taylor, that rotten scoundrel, never should have been trusted. His allures, handsome face and knowledge of her world were nothing more than a trap.

Eterna was no longer there with her, she had to survive on her own and bring this criminal to justice.

Motivation made her lift her paws and wobble to her feet. Each foot seemingly had a mind of its own but she quickly united them. She shuffled her feet, sliding her front feet forward and then the back ones. She stretched like an accordion as she made her way across the forest. Her feet patterns seemed quite easy once she got used to it, but she heard a sickly growl and began to slink along faster.

She wished she had Eterna to guide her walking. Her new body was cumbersome, and who better to teach her than the great Wyrmwolf herself?

She heard distant growls that made her pick up her feet. She forgot about moving each individual foot and just moved them as a whole. It was like the last time she fled from danger, running away from a beautiful but violent man.

She was heading deeper and deeper into the dark forest. It was a forest rife with danger of all kinds, not just Wyrmwolf spirits, but other menaces.

She heard voices spoken in a tongue she could recognize.

"I think we should devour Old Wing," a voice hissed.

"We are hungry and our children are hungrier. It's not fair that soul fruit is so hard to find," another growled. "If we are to survive, sacrifices are to be made."

Aya didn't know if she should head towards the voices or away from them, but soon she lost all sense of direction and ran smack into another Wyrmwolf.

She tasted dirt, gravel and withered grass as she tumbled aside the beast she crashed into. The confused Aquan looked up, still dazed, but with enough wits to still perceive things. The dark purple Wyrmwolf she had ran into flapped a singular wing in order to get himself aligned with the ground, but it was no use with only one. He crawled back to his feet with a certain misery.

"Who is this beautiful silver Wyrmwolf? She has the presence of the elder herself," A voice creaked from the depths of the forest.

Aya could only see its eyes in the mire of darkness.

"She looks good," another voice salivated, "made of prime meat, tender but juicy and probably not as stale as Old Wing."

Aya looked around as Wyrmwolves stepped forward; their eyes dulled with hunger and their mouths hanging open with drool pouring out. Their ribcages jutted out, seemingly banging on their skin, demanding to be fed.

Aya thought fast.

She let her instincts guide her and linked her paws around the wolf known as Old Wing.

The ravenous beats lunged, flying at the two with predatory speed and precision.

Aya flapped her wings and lifted him up into the air as one of the starved beasts scratched her legs and she whimpered.

Her wings lifted her above the trees into the night sky; but she soon found that Old Wing could not be supported. He was beginning to slip without opposable thumbs to clutch him.

Aya hovered downward back into the forest, hoping to find as much distance between the other Wyrmwolves and them.

They roughly landed back on the ground, surrounded by full darkness once again.

Old Wing rose to his feet and began to nudge Aya with his nose. "Are you okay?"

Aya looked up at him, and he staggered back.

"Is that you Eterna?" he gasped. "Or is cruel fate playing tricks on me?"

"Eterna?" Aya shook her head. "I'm not a Wyrmwolf, I'm an Aquan who has transformed into one."

Old Wing's head dropped down. "Of course you are. No wonder you have those outlandish things hanging on your ears."

"I know Eterna though." Aya returned with a frown. "She is my spirit guide. Who are you?"

Old Wing lowered his paws and rested on the ground. "So Eterna has entered the next stage of her life," the Wyrmwolf grumbled to himself. "So be it. Truly a twisted irony to have been saved by someone in her flesh."

Aya's wolflike eyes opened wide. "Who are you? What is your relation to Eterna?"

Old Wing refused to meet her gaze. "Just a nobody she used to know."

Aya's naturally precocious nature got the best of her. Sticking her nose in Old Wing's face, she responded, "you must have been somebody to her if you're acting like that."

The battered old Wyrmwolf muttered fast and quick in response. "I may have given her a pup."

It was now Aya's turn to take a step back. She lowered her mouth and let out a rumbling growl, taking a powerful stance. "You're that traitorous alpha male she told me about? How could you treat Eterna so badly?"

Old Wing sat up. "Take a walk with me," he beckoned. "I have a story to tell you."

Aya's fur stood up as anger coursed through her veins. Old Wing saw this and bowed in front of her. "Please, I'll never last this night. The others have succumbed to the darkness of the forest. They hunger for flesh of their own kind and believe the weakest links should go first."

"That's horrible," Aya said, her light blue eyes opened wide from the shock. Her face softens and she lowers her head. "I guess I try to turn my eyes away from nature's cruelty. Sometimes it's hard to know what to do as a mediator of all creatures."

"Will you listen to my story?"

"Okay, I'll come with you, but I think you're a lowly wolf for the way you treated Eterna."

"I am a lowly wolf. Always have been, always will be." His singular wing folded as the two Wyrmwolves walked the forest, following the glowing blue rot on the trees.

"Listen," he said, "I don't know what Eterna told you. But being a power-hungry alpha male cost me greatly. I had a one-on-one fight with Eterna."

"Eterna never told me that," Aya said as she weaved past darkened spirit trees.

"She probably didn't tell you that at the height of her powers, she was the most fearsome fighter in the forest," Old Wing choked out. "I was foolish to…go up against her." He paused and mustered up his will to continue. "We clashed and she wounded me worse than I could have imagined," the Wyrmwolf growled and swung his left front claw violently. "My right wing was torn up amongst a fury of teeth and claws."

As Aya took heed to Old Wing's words, she began to realize other things about Old Wing. There was a slightly swollen scar cut under his right eye and he walked with a limp. Combined with the missing wing, he looked worse for wear.

The miserable Wyrmwolf continued. "I will let you in on the trade since you're new to being a Wyrmwolf. Our wings are our biggest sign of pride. They are the symbol of countless cycles of evolution."

Old Wing peered out from behind his sodden eyes into Aya's crystal blue ones. "For an Alpha to lose even one of his wings…it outright removes him from any position of respect and leadership."

Aya was silent. She just sized up the tormented creature that stood in front of her. "I spent years wandering aimlessly when I could have very much been known as the mate of the great Eterna." His body lowered in sorrow. "I underestimated her in every way because I was an arrogant fool."

He looked at Aya expecting a harsh condemnation, but when Aya spoke again, she was surprisingly mild in her assessment.

"I won't judge you anymore, Old Wing. You've already suffered you're your crimes. But it's given you the gift of humility. There's another man I know who committed a great crime and will hide it under piles of bodies if he must. You've made the brave choice to be humbled by your sins. You should take pride of that."

"You're wise beyond your years, young Aquan. I wish that…I could apologize to Eterna for everything that I did." Old Wing's voice grew soft. "I gave away the greatest thing I ever laid claim to…her love for me."

The romantic in Aya caused her heart to soften. "Would you like me to tell her that if I ever see her again?"

"Please do," Old Wing said.

"I will," Aya responded and she swore she saw a tear in his eyes, but it was impossible to tell in the dim lighting.

Old Wing began to walk again. "I have something to show you. It's a place we can hide until the night ends."

Aya stood skeptically, hesitant to follow him further into the woods when she had to return to town. She was no longer wary of Old Wing, but she had a duty to protect the village and its people. "I have to save my town."

Old Wing turned around. "If you're talking about that town of humans, I think they'll more likely harm you the way you are now. Come, where I'm going is something that might help you."

Aya hesitated further, but soon accompanied Old Wing.

The tired Wyrmwolf nodded to a nearby tree splattered with a luminous jelly shaped in the form of a crescent. "We'd never get anywhere in this dark forest without the help of some rotten soul fruits I used to mark the trees."

Aya looked onward and saw withered Atma trees with glowing crescent markings.

The Wyrmwolves made their trot, following the seemingly unorthodox order of the marked trees.

"Where is this taking us?" Aya said, after passing the tenth one in yet another direction.

She had begun to feel confused and disoriented from every start and stop they had made. At last, they arrived at the charred remains of the matriarch tree. Its bow was uprooted from collapsing over the fire and electricity Taylor rained on it with his vehicle.

Even in the darkness, Aya could see all the twisted roots that had been tied to the very foundation of the planetoid for centuries.

Aya's heavy brow went up in response. "You really had to make things complicated for us just to come here?"

"Those wolves, their brains are dimmed by hunger. They'd never be able to follow such complex patterns," Old Wing responded.

"Good, I thought you were crazy yourself." Aya laughed.

"Believe me, I was crazier at the height of my alpha male days. It's been a spiral downward to cold harsh sanity since then," the Wyrmwolf spoke. "Now follow me."

Old Wing walked over to the bottom of the tree with its exposed roots and began to dig in the dirt.

Aya watched as he excavated further and further until his paws scraped against wood buried deep within the planetoid's soil.

She ran over and looked at what he had unearthed.

It was a wooden panel that had somehow not burned. The panels were painted with large white symbols, and Aya, a frequent reader of Jeeg's book, recognized it as an ancient Slyphen rune.

Aya's heart sped up at the sight of them.

Sylphens were an elven species on Tarabos who dwelled on a large city known as Argon that was kept afloat by their magic.

While Aya's magic allowed her control over water, Sylphens abilities were masters of levitation.

Inside their magical city, they were tasked with keeping and collecting the records of the planet, something neither the sea shell dwelling Aquans nor nomadic Acridians did much of.

The leveling of Argon alongside the planet of Tarabos itself guaranteed that most of the philosophical, religious works and even lesser stories and poems of the Aquans, Acridians and Sylphens would be gone forever.

"This is amazing," she said, her voice breathy. "It didn't burn."

Old Wing shook the dirt out of his dusty paws. "This wood seems to be enchanted, but that's not the amazing part."

He bit the latch on the paneled door and pulled it aside, revealing lilywhite stone steps underneath the tree, leading into the catacombs.

Further gnarled roots from the tree could be seen twisting inside the tunnel as Old Wing and Aya stepped down the cold pale steps. They possessed the same white glow of the matriarch tree but they were fading, no longer connected to their primal source of life.

The shriveling roots convulsed with sickly exhaling, like they were an asthmatic failing to control an attack on their lungs. It conjured up nothing but pity and sadness for Aya as she moved through the tunnel.

"Where are we going?" she asked as curiosity filled her mind.

"We're going to my resting place," Old Wing said as they turned the corner and the passage way expanded, coming to a large gate formed out of white vines that twisted and turned around each other in perfect discipline. Like the roots, their breath could be heard. It was less sickly, but just as tense. "Hold up. You can still fight on. Maybe Jeeg can heal you."

"Just follow me, Aquan."

Aya practically galloped on her four feet when she saw what it was. "Nature's gate!"

"Hopefully this can help you out," the grizzled Wyrmwolf spoke in return.

She began to cautiously sniff around it with her nose as the air filled with white fog, almost like there was dry ice nearby. She called out to the gate, hoping for a response.

"Nature's Gate, I am humbled in your presence. You may not be acquainted with me, but I am Aya Tintel, the successor of Eterna."

A vine unraveled itself from one of the many tangled bars and lashed at Aya's foot. She gave a loud bark in surprise and jumped back before another vine came up behind her and wrapped around her foot. The guardian nipped at it, but her attempts were futile as she was slowly hoisted upward by the vine. She began to struggle as she was lifted up higher and higher to the center of the gate.

Vines shaped into the form of a toothy mouth expanded before her and began to slide back and forth. A voice reverberated as deep and thick as one who possessed a mile-long windpipe.

"Such an impetuous young creature. You lack the humility in the presence of a century old being. You do not speak unless first spoken to."

Aya realizing her mistake, hung limp and bowed her head. "I am sorry, Nature's Gate. Please accept my apology."

More vines released from the gate and wrapped around her other feet so she remained situated in the air. Moving closer, she felt a presence that belonged as much to the planetoid as to the deities that existed in an intangible plane.

The mouth of the gate wrinkled in disgust. "Benevolent one will do. It is how I've judged your people until now, until a humanoid brought destruction against my motherly bow."

Aya's head reared towards the mouth, and her voice though growling tried to plea with the will of nature. "No one who lived on this planet's soil is to blame. An outsider, not even from this planet hastily destroyed your tree."

The voice creaked and groaned as its vines twisted into a face of anguish. "Assigning the blame to one soul shall not undo the suffering of all those who live upon this planetoid. It has become everyone's responsibility."

"They don't deserve it," Aya said in a voice high and fragile for a wolf. "Why must everyone suffer for one man's crime?"

The gate breathed deeply and Aya could feel the moisture expose itself from the vines. It cooled her, but also made her feel damp and soggy.

The gate spoke again. "Nature and life itself hang from a strong chord, but once that chord is severed, it may never be mended again. No matter who commits the crime, it affects everyone."

"Surely there's something we can do," Aya said as light from the glowing vines caught in her eyes. "We already have seeds from the matriarch tree."

"Your idealism is all but admirable," the voice creaked. "A new tree can only be grown from deep within the planetoid's core. It must grow from the planetoid's mind drive."

"The mind drive?"

The gate of vines breathed deeply again before expelling many words. "Aquan who has become my new guardian, do you wish to know the root of this planetoid's existence?"

"Yes, I am ready, O benevolent one."

"I reside deep within the core of the planetoid. I am the planetoid's mind drive, the planetoid's innermost thoughts," said the ancient voice. "Every living thing born here is tied to me, they can only pass once their spirit is fully purified. When they are hurt, I share in their agony."

"So, you must regenerate from the core? What can I do to help it along?"

The mind drive was silent for an indefinite period of time. "It is best for the humans to go," it declared. "The planetoid should have one caretaker to perform the rituals associated with the growth of the matriarch tree but the rest will only taint the planet further."

"But where should they go?" Aya continued to question.

She didn't wish to uproot all of the farmers from their longtime home.

The gate was definite and firm in its intentions and the normally argumentative Aya never challenged it. "I cannot answer that. Nature must rebuild what they have destroyed. It is no longer safe for the humans here. Their food sources have withered and the true denizens have become hostile. Do you understand?"

Aya nodded her head slowly. She was unable to process everything, so she let her mouth hang open until her wits were organized. "I'll do whatever I can to help everyone."

The next time the gate spoke, it seemed pleased by Aya's words. "Seeing a humanoid desire to carry out my will fills me with gratitude."

Aya sensed that the time was now to ask the gate about herself. She had finally gotten on its good side. "Please, your benevolence, just tell me one thing."

"What is it, young one?"

"Please explain my nature of becoming a beast," said Aya. "I have no idea how it happened and I want to return to my Aquan form."

"When you fused with a nature born guardian," the gate said, "you allowed your form to become neither humanoid nor beast. You are now a demi-goddess and your body no longer responds to wounds the same way it once did."

"How did you know I was wounded?" Aya inquired, feeling frail and confused.

"You obviously became a Wyrmwolf by mistake," the all-knowing presence responded. "When one of Tarabos has fused with nature, they gain two bodies—elf and beast— and when one body is damaged the other retreats into a pocket to recover and you change to your unused body."

"But how do I change back?" asked Aya, praying she'd see her other form again.

"You must use a piece a refined spirit wood that has chosen you as its master," the voice said. "It is what allows the transfer of forms."

Aya's eyes opened wide and her response was flustered and desperate. "My staff. I need to get it back. Ugh… how on Tarabos am I going to do all of this?"

She began to shake her head in pain. She was beginning to feel an overload in her brain from the ever-burdening number of tasks on her back. She felt more cooling from the vines, releasing a brisk and mellow feeling into her. The vines loosened slightly binding Aya's feet and the voice began to talk in a more caring and fatherly way. "Your ancestors who once resided here have put heavy belief in a youthful Tarabosian who has fused with nature. They prophesized that he or she will one day inherit the mind drive."

"Inherit? What do you mean inherit?" Aya intoned softly.

"Their words, not mine," the now gentle voiced gate spoke. "But know that they believed it is your youthful love for the planetoid that will allow me to prosper once more. You will inherit the mind drive."

Tears flowed from Aya's eyes but they were tears of a long held-in-but-now-released stress. She felt her body being slowly lowered by the vines. "Rest, and tomorrow you will be ready to face this world again," they said to Aya.

"Wait up, will I ever find true love? You're all-knowing right?"

The mind drive laughs and the walls shake. "Ah Aquan, I cannot see the future. You are a great soul that deserves love. That much I am fully certain of. You should look around and notice those who already love you."

Aya blushed bright pink. "Thank you. I'm honored."

"Oh…but love is not something you should burden yourself with. A guardian must cherish all life equally."

"Yes, I know that. I…thank you for your wisdom," said Aya softly, doubt in her eyes.

Aya touched the ground and slowly walked over to Old Wing. She walked and nuzzled her snout against his body before lying down.

"What was that for?" he asked, dumbfounded and a bit startled.

"You just looked so soft to me. Like a fluffy pillow. Sorry! Goodnight," Aya said as she laid her head down abruptly.

Old Wing could hardly process what happened; but considering his connections with Eterna, he moved a small distance from her before settling down himself. "Goodnight, Aya."

For the rest of the night, under the protection of nature's gate, Aya slept peacefully. She laid her troubles aside along with her worries of finding romance. Her dreams circled around a single matter: her inheritance of the mind drive.

PUP AYA

Chapter 9

What did inheriting the mind's drive mean? Would that be the only way to rejuvenate the Planetoid? It wasn't until the end of her final dream that she moved past these worrisome thoughts. She knew she had many challenges ahead of her and decided instead to focus on those. She had to find a way to return to her true state of body. Only then would she be able to speak to the villagers and take down Taylor's fog of deception.

Aya awoke without knowing the exact time of day. Not only was she deep in an underground sanctuary, but that place was in a forest where the spirit trees kept out most of the sunlight. She would have to escape the forest before discerning how much time had passed.

She rolled over from her back and saw Old Wing sleeping with his paws stretched out, one providing a pillow for his head. He mumbled and whined in his sleep much like a human would do.

Aya listened closely and heard him breathing in and out again while saying one word: "Eterna…"

Aya couldn't help but manage a small giggle at him.

Hearing her giggle, he awoke with a start, shuffling to his feet with his wings flapping. He gave a worried expression that made Aya feel a bit guilty. "Were you laughing at me?"

"Sorry," she said quickly. "I didn't want to wake you. Wyrmwolves are just funny sleepers."

"I could say the same for you uh…" he glared at her but as he glared his eyes softened and he muttered, "just forget it. Don't you need to get your staff back?"

"Yes," Aya said. "If you could help me get it, it'd be much appreciated."

"What do you want me to do?"

Aya moved her paw forward and trailed it along the floor of the catacombs. "Just back me up when we enter the village. We need to gain intel on where my staff is located."

"I shall assist however I can," the purple Wyrmwolf said, standing up straight.

"You might need to back me up too if they spot us, but let's try our best to avoid confrontation."

The two Wyrmwolves left Nature's Gate and proceeded up the stony steps. They were greeted by the same stillborn wilderness they had left the following night.

Even with the withered trees, sunlight poked through the forest, letting them know it was daytime. Both slinked through the forest, heading from one Atma tree to the next in order to avoid any pursuers. The forest was strangely still and barren until Aya turned the corner of one Atma tree and found an empty eyed carcass of a yellow streaked thunder boar buzzing with hungry flies.

She gasped before bowing her head in sorrow. "Looks like it just keeled over," said Old Wing.

"We need to regenerate this planetoid before this sacred place becomes a bog," Aya said, rising with determination.

They saw a streak of gold in the distance and, soon after, they emerged from the forest into the sunlight.

Both squinted at first, but as soon as they adjusted, Aya lead Old Wing straight to their town.

Aya found it hard to creep along the grass and dirt. Her paws and sharp claws pressed across the dirt with a dry but distinct sound. She walked up against the shadows of a nearby cabin and peered around the edge. She heard soft chattering in the distance coming from the beer barn.

"I hear humans," Old Wing said in her ear, making her jump. He was much better at creeping silently and had moved from the grass hill right to where she was.

"Don't scare me like that," she growled, causing him to flinch.

She realized her mistake and quickly apologized. "I'm sorry, Old Wing. I'm going to listen and see if I can make out the conversation."

Aya closed her eyes and the mumbling became clear to her. The voices became very distinct, not just because of her enhanced Wyrmwolf hearing, but because she knew exactly who they belonged to.

"Lovely day we're having, Flora. And it makes you bloom like a flower in the sun."

"Please, Mr. Lunsford. Call me Miss Du Bois. Daddy makes it a point that men should be formal around me."

"Oh, not a problem, Miss Du Bois." Taylor's voice lowered as he said 'Du Bois'. "Your dad was nice enough to introduce me to you and your mom set us up a nice lunch of sliced fruit too. I really feel welcomed here." He looked at her forlorn expression. "What's on your mind? You look troubled."

"Oh, just that mom shouldn't have made us such a nice lunch when we really should be conserving our fruit. We only have a few months of left of supplies and more fruit doesn't seem to be growing."

"Hey, live in the now, sunflower. I'm sure they're coming up with a solution at this very moment in the beer barn."

Flora's delicate voice became sharp. "I said call me Miss Du Bois."

"Right. Is that really all that's troubling you?"

"I uh…" Flora's voice retreated back to soft and vulnerable, "I just can't stop worrying about Aya."

"She's in the forest, like I said. She said she wanted to do some mystical, nature stuff. That's what she told me. I think she wants to soothe that rogue flying wolf thing that attacked me last night."

"I know, I saw the Wyrmwolf. I just thought Aya'd be back by now."

"You saw it?!" Taylor's voice leapt an octave before becoming very quiet and mumbled so Aya couldn't hear it.

"Yeah, I saw that Wyrmwolf on top of you. I was so concerned. I would have probably have passed out from shock."

The theatrics Flora used surprised Aya greatly, and she wasn't sure if Flora was putting on an act. All she knew is she wanted to learn more about what Flora saw.

Taylor's voice rose up again to its usual deep brashness. "You really have a feminine softness to you. That's a cherished rarity these days. Your friend Aya could learn a thing from you."

"I quite like the way she is. She has a way with nature that is quite mystifying. She just swings her staff and things feel more relaxed for all of us. That's why I was so curious how she could soothe nature without it."

"Without it? Doesn't she have her staff?" Taylor said, trying to play dumb.

"No, I found it floating in the sea by where the beast attacked you." Flora's normally flighty and high voice suddenly became sly and even a bit taunting. "Don't worry, I kept it safe where no one can find except me and her."

"Oh, you girls and your secret places. I bet I can get you to tell me where it is." Taylor tried to remain relaxed and cool but cracks in his façade were showing.

"Nope. Not telling. Nu-uh."

"Don't be such a tease," Taylor said. "I thought farm girls were supposed to be simple-minded and sweet."

"I don't think any girl is as simple as you think, Mr. Lunsford."

"I've met plenty."

Aya knew exactly where this secret place was and realized she had an edge over Taylor. She motioned to Old Wing to follow her as they ran along the edge of the village. She counted herself lucky that they had decided to have a town meeting about the state of the town. Not a single person walked the streets. No children playing, no women doting after them, no farmers bringing their spoils home in a burlap sack, the place was free for two Wyrmwolves to cross safely.

Aya was reminded of the need to evacuate everyone from their home, kicking up dust as she ran. She knew as soon as she became a humanoid again, she'd have to convey the planetoid's wishes to everyone, whether they liked it or not.

Old Wing trailed after her, his worn-out leg limping along and slowing him down considerably.

Aya reached the outskirts where a small dilapidated hut stood. Its formerly white spirit wood had faded to a dull, water-stained grey. Such was the result of using non-refined spirit-wood. Despite this, Aya had sentimental feelings towards this hut.

She remembered two little girls, an Aquan and a ginger haired human playing in it for the first time. For the farmers, it was an abandoned storehouse that had long out of use by the two-story beer-barn; but for two children, it was anything they imagined. Aya pretended it was a sea-shell castle, similar to the one belonging to the king of the Aquans. Flora pretended it was a spaceship taking them to far off destinations. Most often she consented with her friend that it was better off a castle because of Aya's traumas from space.

Aya knew the staff was in the place her and Flora hid special objects in their childhood: their little hut.

She pushed her snout against the door, but quickly realized in animal form she'd never open anything that way. She decided to take a few steps back, lining up with the door and readying herself to take an enormous charge at it. She began to dash on her four legs—legs she had become quite used to—with her head lowered at the ground. Seeing a pair of legs, she lifted her head and skidded to a stop. Looking up in fear, she saw Taylor armed with his red dagger ready to cut her throat. She let out a loud bark.

"How did he find us?"

She blamed Old Wing for taking a long time to follow her as they ran through the village, but she didn't say it out loud.

"Beats me, but if he's an enemy, I'll take him on," Old Wing said, looking to bite Taylor.

Taylor slashed at her, slicing fur just an inch off from her skin. If she hadn't rolled, it would have pierced her through.

In retaliation, Old Wing lunged at him, leaping high at his face.

Taylor ducked, allowing the Wyrmwolf to fly over his head and land with a limp on the ground. "I see you brought your mate," he said, grinning through gritted teeth. "Not a bad catch, though he's nowhere near as handsome as me."

Taylor walked slowly towards Old Wing who was struggling to get up. He was poised to kill, but Aya quickly rushed to Old Wing's aid.

As she ran, she heard voices all around her and soon saw the whole village of about thirty men, women and children surrounding them.

Flora stood at the center of the crowd with a newly sober Du Bois.

Taylor turned around, rage filling his eyes as he screamed. "Flora, what are you doing? There are rabid Wyrmwolves here. I told you to run away when we saw them."

Aya knew the real reason he was angry, but she waited for Flora to speak to confirm it. "Don't let Taylor hurt the Wyrmwolf. She's Aya, I saw her transform last night."

116

Mr. Du Bois turned to his daughter with an incredulous look on his face. "Flora, you told me these Wyrmwolves were attacking Taylor. Now you say one of them is Aya. Good lord, and I thought I had too much to drink last night."

Aya remembered that Flora had run out of the beer barn last night. She supposed her friend had followed her and Taylor down to the freshwater sea. There was plenty of large rocks to hide behind over there. She thanked the creator she had a guardian as sweet as Flora watching over her.

The townsfolk rumbled with disbelief and Du Bois spoke again to Flora.

"My daughter, if I were you, I would stand down and lie in bed. You're clearly having one of your dizzy spells. Just let us take care of these Wyrmwolves. They have been going mad lately."

Mr. Du Bois drew a blade himself, but Flora quickly ran out in front of him with her arms outstretched. "Please daddy, you never listen to me. You never listen to me about anything! I do try to keep an eye on Jaz and I don't want to be married to a man. Please, you never listen. Just listen, this one time."

Mr. Du Bois, a man very rarely flustered stood in silence as Flora ran towards Aya who was still in the mood to tear Taylor limb from limb. She growled at Flora accidentally, causing her to flinch with a loud squeak. "Flora," Mr. Du Bois called, "somebody stop her."

He looked to Allons and Gully who flanked him, but both (and especially the latter who had just gotten over a large Wyrmwolf fright of his own) hid behind him.

Aya began to approach Flora instead as the girl began to mutter. "It's okay. She's not going to hurt me. She's my friend. She's not a beast. She's not going to hurt me."

"Taylor, save my daughter from that beast," Du Bois ordered and Taylor began to walk towards Aya. He was almost there when Old Wing took a bite out of Taylor's leg, causing him to howl in pain, and clumsily swing at Old Wing. He missed and fell flat as the wizened wolf ran off, scaring some villagers in the process as they parted to let him escape.

No longer bothered by Taylor, Aya approached Flora who had turned pale as a sea lily. Her chest began to convulse as past incidents tortured her mind.

Aya looked straight up at the trembling woman and let out a gentle whine.

Flora looked right at the beast, right into her bright blue eyes and saw the long brown jewelry hanging off her Wyrmwolf ears. "Aya?" She asked with a voice so thin and frail.

Aya ran her nose against Flora's sundress and the girl reached her arm out and scratched behind Aya's ears. Her Wyrmwolf wings that had become outstretched in excitement, suddenly retracted back to their resting position, and Aya began to relax.

Flora crouched down and said, "Look everyone, this Wyrmwolf has the same earrings as Aya. That pup is Aya!"

Jeeg quickly crept from the crowd over to Aya and Flora and crouched beside them. "It is as she said. I'd know that fashion sense anywhere."

Flora's eyes lit up. "Pup, Aya. Wow! Pupaya! She always did love fruit!"

Du Bois still looked like he didn't believe Jeeg and Flora, but he had to be careful with the beast so close to his daughter. "So, if this beast really is Aya? Can she turn back into an earian?"

Aya barked loudly as Du Bois, still scorned from that word he often used, but Jeeg quickly settled her. "There there, calm down, Aya."

Flora's eyes lit up like a beacon. "Oh by golly, she came to our secret place for her staff. Maybe that can change her back. Jeeg, can you get it?"

She motioned to the door. The old man walked inside and rummaged through the old shack. He emerged with her staff in hand.

Aya stood up and began panting frantically. Her heart raced. This was the moment of truth.

She reached up and bit the staff. It began to glow brightly as it entered her maw. She closed her eyes and soon was hit with a vision of a tan skinned baby with long ears, wrapped tightly in a blanket. A younger Jeeg held the baby and gave her to two Aquans- A handsome elven man with long flowing wine-colored hair, and a beautiful elven woman with large blue eyes and short scruffy bob.

Aya could feel her body stretch as her Wyrmwolf body fell on the ground. Her nose retracted back to being humanoid size, her ears shifted back to the side of her head. Her body returned from the animalistic shapes of a Wyrmwolf to the curves of a female humanoid.

The Aquan opened her eyes and saw Flora looking down at her, her face was bright red and Jeeg with a smile said, "You're back."

There were some whistles and cries from the crowd at her return.

Aya rose to her bottom and looked at her arm. Upon it was Eterna, giving her a sad frown. "I'm sorry I went against your word, Eterna. I let my guard down. I should have been stronger," she pleaded.

Eterna continued to frown. "You're a child," said the tattooed Wyrmwolf with closed eyes. "A wild little child with a lot of spunk. I was just trying to help you avoid my mistakes, but experience is a better mentor than I."

"I promise it won't ever happen again!" Aya exclaimed with a bow and a smile.

"You might want to put on some clothes," Eterna said laughing. "You're awakening the carnal lust in these so-called civilized men."

Gully whispered to Allons as they continued to leer at her. "This would be attractive if she wasn't talking to one of her tattoos like a madwoman."

"Well, I think it's pretty dern hot anyway," said Allons, fanning himself with his straw-hat before being pulled off by his angry wife.

Mrs. Du Bois ran over to Aya and put a large cloth around her. "I'm sorry about those wretched excuses for men. I'm just happy my daughter spotted you when she did."

"I'm thankful too," Aya said, looking up at her friend who continued to be as red as a ripe tomato. "Flor, you're the best. And I never knew you were so resourceful."

Flora straightened her frayed hair and fixed her large sun hat. She smiled back bashfully. "I saw Taylor and you fighting and then you just transformed. I was too scared to charge right in and...I thought I lost you. When I found you again, I didn't fear Wyrmwolves or anything…I just had to protect you."

Aya stood up and put her clothed arm around her friend. "You were wonderfully brave. Just a few days ago you were afraid of a baby Wyrmwolf. Today you faced down two adult wolves and a madman. You're always reliable when it matters."

Flora jumped and Aya turned around to see Taylor grinning with his hand on their shoulders. He winced a little. His leg was bleeding from where Old Wing bit him. He continued to put up his façade, but not only were Flora and Aya on to his routine, some of the villagers looked at him sternly.

"I can't believe that crazy beast was Aya. It's a good thing Flora told us all the truth. I'm honestly more upset with myself than you are. But I did rescue that little girl, so I'll learn to forgive myself."

Flora turned around and shoved Taylor, raising her high voice to an angry pitch that Aya rarely heard. She was clearly high on the adrenaline from the whole incident. "Save it, Mr. Good Hair. I saw the whole scene right down to where you stabbed my best friend before she became a wolf."

Taylor put his hands behind his back and gave an angelic smile to the crowd. "Stabbing? I'd never do such a thing to Aya. I think Mr. Du Bois is right, Flora, I think you should lie down. This whole experience has been a shock for us all."

Aya turned around with a sad look on her face. "Flora speaks true."

She lifted her cloth and pointed at the left side of her stomach. There was only a faint scar. The healing in the spirit pocket had done wonders, but it had not recovered the full wound.

"You do realize if I had stabbed you, there would be a gashing hole in your stomach," Taylor said, mimicking agonizing pain.

The crowd rumbled. Some were in Taylor's favor, some not, until Mr. Du Bois stepped forward.

"I'm the leader of this town and I...think my daughter was seeing things again. There's no way that wound could have healed overnight."

Flora's pale face shot back into tomato territory as she began to scowl and make a horrible wordless screech at her father. She crossed her arms and turned away from him to Taylor. She thought for a second before speaking again. "What made that mark on her, then?"

Taylor's deep voice, smug and conceited came up with an immediate answer. "She always had that. I'm sure it's a birthmark. Oh, well she also runs along the forest. It's easy to be cut by a stray branch or mad beast."

Aya removed her whole robe to more caws from the rude townsfolk and gasps from mothers shielding their children's eyes. She wrapped it around her lower body and covered her chest. "I display my tattoos with pride. It's who I am. You see my midriff fishes daily, but has anyone ever seen that dark mark on me before?"

Taylor swallowed hard. He realized that the way Aya dressed gave the opportunity for many of the male townsfolk to leer at her well-cut stomach. They may not have been super sleuths or master detectives; but like Taylor, Aya knew where their eyes would be drawn most.

"Yeah, Aya's darn tootin. I'd remember seeing that scar while we were out farming," Allons said again, breaking into the crowd as his wife grabbed him and dragged him off again.

"Exactly," Aya said with a confident bounce. "And, if you don't believe me, Du Bois, how about we do this?"

Aya grabbed the cuff of Taylor's wrist and twisted it. He screamed and dropped his knife. She scooped it up and positioned it right at her stomach. "Take a good look, Du Bois. It's exactly the same size."

Du Bois bent over and squinted, observing the knife's perfect trajectory with the mark. "Hmm, I think I'm going to have to retract my accusation." He turned to Taylor with a look of utter scorn on his face. "Men, seize him."

Taylor with a look of abject horror began to limp away, but soon felt the weight of several farmers piling onto him. He was lifted to his feet by two of the burliest fruit hoisters in town and Du Bois pointed to the beer barn. "Once you get him tied down, I want to question him personally. We were having a dire meeting before this distraction."

Du Bois looked Taylor right in the eyes and howled in his rural dialect. "Boy, I'm extremely disappointed in you! You have gone from a hero to a lowly scoundrel in the course of two days."

Taylor was silent as he was carried off. Du Bois signaled to the townsfolk with his good hand. "Now that that's over. We can continue this meeting concerning the future of the village. Aya, Flora, you're welcome to join too."

With that, Du Bois walked away surrounded by every member of the village.

She had to tell everyone the truth about the incident with the Great Spirit Tree. Aya was bewildered at Mr. Du Bouis finally being helpful to her. She hoped this would allow her to convince the villagers about and what she had been told by the mind core. That in order to not lose their planetoid they would have to leave it.

First, she had to make a quick stop at her cabin to get dressed. She knew she must look her best during this upcoming meeting of monumental importance.

DANCE OF THE SPIRITS

Chapter 10

Aya sat down and crossed her hands. "Are you really planning on going into that forest alone? It's haunted by wolfhound spirits! They have no eye for friend or foe, only a blinding rage."

Jeeg nodded. "It is my duty. Just as you have your responsibilities, I have mine."

Aya gave a shiny white fanged smile. "I can't sit around and fiddle while an old codger risks his neck in the forest! If something happened to you…I'd be so upset with myself for not coming along!"

Eterna speaks up. "Please, it is too much of a burden for an old one. Let her help."

Jeeg lowered his head. "It's because I'm old that I want to do this. Aya, you are too important. I've already taught you everything I can."

Aya stands up in protest. "Well, I won't allow it! You're a part of this Planetoid! I'm sworn to protect everyone!"

Taylor raises his head, tied up in the back of the room. "Hello, you can always ask moi for some incredible feats of daring!"

Aya glares. "No!"

Jeeg chuckles. "We want to quell the spirits, not enrage them."

Aya grins. "Perhaps a sacrifice would appease them. I mean, he is responsible after all."

Taylor nods, still tied up. "Yes, I'm very responsible." He sighs. "Okay, enough bravado. I want to make amends for my mistake. I want to help, Aya."

Aya shrugs. "You just want to escape."

Taylor speaks tenderly. "Only so I can be with you, great Aquan."

Jeeg stands in front of him when he notices Aya blushing. "Aya, we leave at once."

Aya blinks confused. "Oh, did I win you over?"

Jeeg closes his eyes. "There is just something left for me to teach you. We will discuss on the way. One last adventure with me, you must be honored."

Aya grins and pokes his arm. "Just admit you need me."

Jeeg nods and smiles back. "Now and always."

Aya couldn't help but grin from pointed ear to pointed ear. Jeeg had cared for her so long that it would mean the whole planetoid to her to work with him.

The guardian Aquan turned to face Flora and her family. "Keep the scoundrel imprisoned and maybe just maybe, he'll realize the damage he's done."

"Sure thing, Aya," Flora said in her sweet drawl. And she took her heel and stomped Taylor's foot.

"Yowch!!!"

Aya and Jeeg make their way deep into the forest.

"You can't be serious," Aya remarked, blushing a gentle pink.

But her curiosity was piqued all the same. She had known of many techniques to calm and quell spirits, but dancing was a brand new one…and very Jeeg.

"Well then," Jeeg rasped proudly. "Let me show you!"

The spritely old man pranced into the forest as Aya rushed to catch him. She was already annoyed about being lured into a dance with that scoundrel, Taylor Lunsford. But this one was with old Jeeg. He didn't have a mean bone in his body, as old as they were.

Inside the darkened grove, Jeeg thrust his fingers forward. "That there looks like a great dance partner for me to show off my moves."

Aya narrowed her eyes. "A bush?"

Jeeg laughed. "You must look beyond."

Aya heard a soft whining sound coming from the shrubbery. Her stomach twisted in knots. It sounded like the ghost wolfhound pup they had come across. Its whines were truly saddening and eerie to the young elven woman.

Sure enough, another transparent wolfhound pup passed through the bushes. Aya readied her staff in case there was a vicious attack. Jeeg, however, struck a pose that more resembled a dance move than a fighting stance. "Stand down, my young protege," he advised Aya. "There is no need for that. Lower your staff and prepare."

"For what exactly?"

"For a dance…of empathy!"

Jeeg tapped his staff and enveloped it in light blue energy. "First, you purify…then…"

Aya's fanged mouth opened in amazement as Jeeg struck a pose and the light blue energy transferred to his body. He had become the embodiment of positive healing energy.

The figure moved with sensuous grace, like Old Jeeg was a demi-god of dance.

The motion, which seemed to be from another world, memorized the little wolfhound spirit. The negative fire red glow that engulfed it slowly turned to a placid blue.

The ghostly beast, once vicious, now had shimmering eyes as it moved along with the purifier. Aya watched for minutes until the energy-filled Jeeg finished his pose. Then her eyes widened as the purified ghost began to ascend to another plane, the tempest in its heart had ceased to stir.

The great purifying dancer spirit now returned to the humble old Jeeg.

Aya clasped her hands together. "I can't believe you waited this long to show me that, old man."

Jeeg laughed. "I had planned to teach you later on. However, now that you've seen the fabulous power of dance, I want you to continue the lineage of Aquan spirit dancers! A dance that has you surrender and become a vessel for the spirit particles around you!"

Aya shook her head. "I'm not sure I can learn this. I have problems, letting someone else steer my will."

Her wolfhound tattoo stuck her head out proudly. "Please child," Eternal asked. "Help my kin with this old coot's unconventional methods. Before we depart, we must heal my people."

Aya was uncertain, but hearing the wolf mother's wise and proud voice made her want to help all these besieged spirits all the more. Especially when she thought of Eterna's pup. She didn't want him to end up like all the lost spirits.

"I'll learn this wacky dance," Aya said, at last. "So I can master nature's rhythm!"

Jeeg grinned widely. Looking quite goofy with his missing teeth, yet still unbelievably loveable. He humbly bowed. "Well," he said. "It all starts with a wiggle of your hips."

The old man shook his tail bone convincingly. "Then you pick a purification spell. What you do is, try to move like the creature."

He opened his mouth and snarled, holding his head high.

"See. I was just impersonating the great majestic wolfhound." Jeeg grinned. "You must do this with all animals you have to purify so I hope you can relive your days of pretend as a kid. You already have a wolfhound spirit in you, Aya. Let her run around and have fun."

Eterna chuckles. "I've heard Aya howl. It's quite cute."

Aya rolled her eyes. "Let's just think of this as playtime before the big mission."

Jeeg smiles with pride. "Yes, that's the spirit!"

Aya started strolling through the forest, very happy nobody but Jeeg would see her acting so childish.

However, as she approached a small pond something bubbled up from the depths.

A ghostly spirit rose from the water.

With vacant, black marble eyes, spiky purple fur and enormous buck teeth, Aya realized the first animal she'd be impersonating was an oversized aquatic rodent known as the Ceaver. With an enormous spiked tail, it could chip down trees with the greatest of ease. It was mostly docile unless you went near its dam.

It chittered needlessly, unaware that it was part of the forests curse.

Jeeg cackled loudly. "Hope you brought your buck teeth, my apprentice. Or buck fangs!"

Aya's arms sunk.

She summoned the purifying spell in her staff. It shined bright purple to match the Ceaver.

And then, the Ceaver began to shake. Aya and Jeeg watched strangely as the ghost of the Ceaver grew bigger and bigger.

"Ummm..." Aya said, looking incredibly nervous. "What kind of dance is this?"

As the Ceaver grew to the size of a large oak tree, Jeeg gulped. "I don't think this is a mere Ceaver ghost."

The beast let out a massive roar as its maw stretched open. Hundreds of spirits of Wolfhounds, Tacoons, Ceavers and other mammals screamed from inside of its black hole mouth.

Jeeg gulped. "T-t-his is the mother of the forest curse!"

Aya's knees trembled as a ghoulish air filled the forest, freezing trees and flowers around them.

"G-good news, protege!" Jeeg lisped through his wrinkled mouth.

"What?" Aya asked.

"T-the good news is," the old man muttered. "If we purify this thing, we purify the whole forest. Dance on her head and we will be home free for a while!"

"That's great." Aya said softly.

Jeeg grabs her hand. "Yes, it is. Now run for your life!"

The pair of Aquans, apprentice and teacher, made a mad dash through the forest as the ghostly beast tore after them. As it moved, it froze everything in its path. From bodies of water, to trees and other plants to even animals. It seemed not to care about the path of destruction it left as long as it captured the interlopers.

Aya ran with the natural ease of youth, but for the elderly Jeeg, it took a toll on his body. He puffed and panted as they weaved around trees. "Protege, I don't know if I'm...gonna make this one!"

"N-n-no!" Aya screamed as Jeeg took a tumble with a final gasp.

She stopped and ceased the old man's body as he plummeted scooping him up in her arms. Due to her natural fitness and diet of spirit fruits, his body was light.

"I have to stop this poor beast!" she cried as she continued to run with Jeeg in her arms. "I have to soothe her ailing soul."

Aya continued to dart back and forth, taking the empty paths to avoid any more souls getting swept up by the ethereal rampage.

The ground rumbled and a massive oak in front of her was ripped out by the roots. As it took a tumble, she sensed that her chance was now.

She carefully ran along the fallen tree, and leaped onto the beast as it lumbered forward. The mother of the curse let out a howl of confusion as Aya had disappeared from her view.

Jeeg slowly opened his eyes as she cradled him like an elderly baby. "Okay, protege. Time to perform the spirit dance."

Aya closed her eyes and nodded.

Her staff was still charged up with purple purifying energy, but she now had to do the dance (with an old codger in her arms no less).

The mother of the forest curse had taken the form of a Ceaver so she now imitated one. She took her fangs and made a stupid bucktooth expression like one of the inbred members of Du Bois family. She then reached out like the beast itself and chittered.

The purple energy flowed through her body like an opened geyser. Her body moved with a placid calm and it overtook her and the beast. Slowly, the beast began to move with her. Aya had never felt a deep oneness with nature of this level before.

A golden white light emanated from inside the beast and the path of destruction it had left in its wake began to bloom with new foliage.

Aya marveled at this phenomenon.

Jeeg muttered, "it seems this wasn't just a curse. This ghost is a protector of the forest. She had just been corrupted. She sought you out, bringing in all the wayward spirits so you could pacify them all."

The beast lowered Aya and Jeeg down gently in a bed of flowers. It had now taken the shape of a golden glowing wolfhound.

Even at her age, Aya couldn't help but still marvel at the wonders of nature.

"You have done well, child!" Eterna said from her tattoo.

"I was just a vessel…" Aya said softly. "Jeeg taught me everything I know."

Jeeg laughed. "But without your talent, kid, none of this would be possible."

"Fine," Aya said, all smiles. "How about it was our teamwork that did it!"

"Agreed!" The old man said. "And now imagine the excitement Miss Flora will have when you share her how we saved the forest."

Aya laughed. "She'll think I'm silly." She looked up at the sky. "But maybe being silly isn't so bad. Thanks to you…I accept my inner child."

Jeeg pats her shoulder. "Don't forget your inner childishness."

As they laughed and chatted about the dangers of men of ill intent, Aya's mind wandered.

"Even if I leave this place, the stories we crafted together, will never leave me."

THE WILD FLOWER

Chapter 11

Flora lied on a futon, cuddling her pillow. Her mind swirled around thoughts of her best friend. She had just set out on another dangerous quest to protect their home. Her eyes opened when she heard a humming sound. She sat up and glared at Taylor.

Noticing her eyes were upon him, Taylor looked her way. "You know," he said with a wiggle of his dashing eyebrows "a wild planet like this is no place for a delicate flower."

Flora covered her mouth and chuckled. "I have lived here all my life. This flower is a wild flower. Hmph!" She turned her nose up at him.

The glint in Taylor's eye signified he wasn't done yet. "Are you sure? I know many planetoids more civilized than this one but few women who match your…"

A loud growl and the stampeding of hooves interrupted his smug diatribe.

Flora rushed outside to see what the commotion was about.

Citizen of the village gasped as large furry creatures of bright yellow charged from the forests and headed straight for the town.

"Thunderboars!" Jaz screamed and cheered, causing everyone to look at her.

"What?!" she answered, striking a valiant pose. "I want to ride one!"

A young orange haired boy about her age stepped forward. He wore corduroy overalls over a hairless bare chest. He was about Jaz's age and he had an equal look of confidence. "Aw Jaz. Leave the boar taming to the men of the village!"

"I don't see any men here, just my dummy brother Buck." Jaz stuck out his tongue.

Flora walked to her siblings and put her hands on their shoulders. "How about instead of fruitless bickering, y'all help me round up some fruit!"

Mrs. Du Bois and her husband had concerned looks over their daughter's bold statement. "Flora, dear. What exactly do you plan on doing?"

Flora put her hands on her banana-green dress. "I'm gonna perform a handy dandy trick I learned from Aya. You see, we jus' need some spirit fruits and...I can...cook up a delicious salad for them!"

Mr. Du-Bois pipe nearly dropped out of his mouth. "You're gonna risk your neck just to feed them beasts?! I wish y'all wouldn't listen to that dagger eared savage.

The loud boars crashed into the huts and tumbled carts of freshly picked vegetables.

Flora turned aside with a loud 'hmph'.

Mrs. Dubious stopped her husband from ranting by grasping his hand and giving him a firm look. "Flora dear. Your father and I are just concerned about you."

"I know that, Ma. But I have to do something. Aya may not be here...but her teachings are." She put her hand to her chest and smiled. "We're gonna pacify those perturbed pudgy piggies with a bountiful bounty of fresh fruits!" She gestured to the sleeping hog in a pile of fruit by the cart.

Mr. Dubois grabs his wife's wrist. "We're wasting time debating her. I'm going to talk to the prisoner. See if he has any ideas."

Mrs. Dubois smiled at her daughter. "And I'll round up some fruit from the vendors."

Flora smiled back and then turned to her siblings. "Soldiers, prepare for battle! We are going to save the village!" She rushed up and grabbed her sibling's hands.

"Wait!" Mr. Du Bois turned around and stifled a grasp, but it was too late. Flora had already headed off.

Mrs. Du Bois an arm around her husband. "Sweetheart, she isn't heading out on a dangerous adventure. She's just making a salad."

Mr. Du Bois sighed. He couldn't fight his wife's words, as much as he wanted to. Flora was a grown woman and she could take care of a few boars.

For civilians, the woods were off limits, especially in the wake of the spirit emergency. Flora had to search for a spirit fruit on the outskirts of the planetoid. Luckily, she had extra eyes to help her search for the tree with the lucky fruit.

"I see it!" Buck exclaimed pointing to the highest tree curved over a crystal blue lake.

"Dangnabbit!" Flora said. "It just had to be a toughie. And to think, I just cleaned this dress too."

Jaz smirked, already partly up the tree. "No worries, Sis, leave this to me! "

"Jaz!" Flora scolded her. "Y'all better be careful."

Buck tried to climb after, but lost his grip and slid down.

Flora caught him. "Buck, let's make a leaf bed, just in case Jaz slips."

"Okay. But I…"

"I know you could do it too."

But Jaz the playful lad had already climbed up on the palm tree, arms wrapped around its base.

Even when Jaz wobbled on the tree, he merely chuckled. "Where's the thrill without a possible spill."

Buck shook his head and looked down. "How is a girl braver than me?"

Flora beams as she watches Jaz go higher and higher, dropping an armful of leaves under the tree. "Jaz has the spirit of a brave warrior burning within!"

Buck wipes his eyes. "And what do I have?"

Flora taps his forehead. "A keen eye! You're going to lead us to all the fruits we need!"

Buck beams and rushes off. "Then I'll go look for more!"

Jaz reached the end of the tree, and began to reach for the glistening morsel.

Flora bit her nails as Jaz reached out.

Jaz's foot slipped and she started sliding down! "Whoa!"

Flora screamed. "Jasmine!"

Jaz stabbed a knife into the tree to stop his momentum. He looks back with a toothy grin. "It's Jaz, Florana."

Flora blushes. "I know I just…"

"I'll prove I'm just as cool as Taylor." Jaz kicked off the tree. He grabbed onto its long leaves.

"Jaz! That's dangerous!" screamed Flora.

"Danger is my breakfast!" Besides, my sweet sister made sure I have a soft landing." Jaz shook the leaves, making the Atma fruits plop down.

"Nicely done. Now don't move. We need to figure out how to get you down safely."

Jaz chuckled. "Aya will just make me a bubble and…"

"Jaz, Aya isn't here."

"Oh." He looked down and his eyes went wide. "Uhh, sis…I'm really really high up." He grabs onto the leaves in terror. "What do I do?"

Buck stands atop a nearby hill. "If you can't catch this, then you have to call me big brother from now on until forever!" He rotates his arm and tosses the fruit. "If you're a real man, then catch it!"

Jaz knocks the fruit with his foot and then catches it in his teeth as it swoops down.

Buck cheers. "Yes! That's my bro! Now, take a bite!"

Jaz bit down and swallowed the super-charged produce. Energy burst through his body like an electrical current.

Jaz swung back and forth on the leaves and then let go. He gripped on the base of the tree and slid down while cheering.

He kicks off and lands in the leaf pile. "Aya's not the only one who can ride the forest!" Jaz backflipped out of the leaves and landed with a split. "Ta-da!!!!"

Buck went to Jaz and slugged his shoulder. "You gotta teach me how to do that, bro."

"Sure thing…as long as you do my chores in a cute maid outfit." Jaz stuck out his tongue.

Flora watched fondly as her brothers playfully chased each other around. "Just like I told Taylor, us Du Bois are wild at heart!"

The trio rushed through the forest back to the Du Bois manor.

Buck offered an apron to Jaz as he adjusted his.

"Ewww. Now way. I don't wanna cook," Jaz complained as they walked backwards.

"Dude, we need your help.".

"Cooking is for girls!" Jaz crossed his arms.

"Umm…" Buck asked nervously. "I like to cook. Does that make me a girl?"

"Only if you wanna be!" Jaz snickered.

Flora placed her hands on both of their shoulders. "Alright Jaz, you can stand guard while Buck and I cook! That's a Tom-manly thing to do!"

Jaz hoisted up a ladle like a sword. "That's perfect. You two girls can cook, while I rough up any ruffian who cares to come through here."

"But I'm not a g…" Buck peeped up, but Flora interrupted him. "Girls love a partner that can cook."

Jaz stops in place. "D-Doesn't matter. I'm gonna protect you pussywillows!" He runs off.

Flora grabs Buck's hand.

"Sis, you don't think cooking is girly, do you?"

"Aww, come on Buck. Boys don't worry what others think right? If you enjoy it then go for it! I always enjoy your cooking and so does Jaz."

Buck grins. "Yeah, he squeals like a little girl when he eats my carroot cake!"

The Du Bois kitchen was the finest cookery on the whole planet. They had managed to procure a working stove, an array of cooking utensils, a heat powered oven and even a hydronic food freezer. Even though Taylor had rendered these machines out-of-date, they still were far more advanced than the kitchens everyone else had. Even though some of the poorer farmers complained, the Du Bois family allowed anyone to use their kitchen.

Jaz patrolled the black-and-white checkered floor with a hup-two-three-four. He looked into the kitchen window with a forlorn gaze.

Buck and Flora laid the fruit out on the chopping table. It glimmered miraculously causing their eyes to shine and glisten in mystification.

Buck beamed. "Wow…they are truly marvelous."

"These fruits," Flora said, "As Aya has told me, are spirit enhancers and calmers. Anyone who has a bite will be more focused, strong and coordinated. These raging piggies will become a herd of sophisticated gentle boars in no time!"

Much to their surprise, Jaz had appeared beside them, her eyes wide with curiosity.

"Hey," Buck said, sticking his tongue out at her. "I thought you were too manly for cooking."

Jaz stuck her tongue back at him. "This isn't cooking! This is survival! Nothing more manly than that."

Flora rolled her eyes. "You two are a handful, y'all know that?"

Removing a salad knife from the wall of cutlery, Flora began to dice the fruit. "Buck, Jaz, can y'all get me some leafy greens."

Buck and Jaz were on it. Jaz went into fridge and retrieved the spinach and the lettuce.

Jaz rolled his eyes. "Are we gonna *boar* them to sleep. These greenies are so bland."

Buck laid out the veggies and Flora's eyes lit up. "This will be perfect. Spinach gives natural energy and will dilute the adrenaline burst from the Atma fruit."

Flora sighed, realizing that Aya would be so proud of her for thinking of the nutrients of the creatures of the planetoid. She'd have a lot to tell her friend when she returned from her spirit pacifying escapade. Flora added diced fruit into the leafy greens and created a fruit salad that any man, woman or beast would find irresistible.

Now was the hard part…feeding it to the raging boars! Flora would need to think of a way to distract them and get them out in the open. She looked at Jaz and Buck with pride.

Flora clasped her hands together. "Everyone, prepare for Operation: Peace Meal!"

Flora peered around the edge of a grass hut in the village. She had the bowl of salad with spirit fruits in her hand. She hoped desperately she made enough to tame the hunger of these wild beasts and soothe the tempest in their souls.

Beside her, was her plan B and her plan J. Together they'd be the tag team trio that saved the day. The beasts were rummaging and charging around the camp like a pack of…well, boars. Some of the huts had been knocked down by the sheer power of their booming thunder stomps. Flora knew she'd have to act quick in order to save the village.

"Go…!" Flora shouted. "Execute plan B!"

"Na na na na na!" a twerpy voice exclaimed. "Thunder boars? More like blunder *bores*!"

Buck pranced through the pathways of the village, drawing the attention of the boars. He turned around and mooned them. Buck continued to laugh until bolts of lightning fired at him. "OH CREATOR, SAVE ME!"

"They're starting to charge…literally!" Flora shouted. "Execute Plan J!"

"Yoo-hoo!" a slightly deeper than Buck's voice called out.

Jaz stood dressed in a flower yellow dress. "Hey, boys. I hear you like frilly and yellow flowers!" He waved his hips side to side in a melodic way.

The boars stopped dead in their tracks and they began to sniff Jaz. He stood timidly, hoping they wouldn't electrocute her.

Instead, one gave her a big lick on her cheek and snorted. "Yuck," Jaz exclaimed. "At least it's better than being kissed by a boy!"

Flora ran out quickly and dropped the bowl of salad behind them. "You got 'em tongue tied and hog tied! That's cuz you're one big electrocutie!"

Jaz couldn't help but blush and turn red.

Buck ran back, fully out of breath. "Whew!" he said. "That saved my bacon!"

The boars grunted. "Err...I mean saved my salad!"

"Speaking of salad," Flora marveled at the boars. "They are loving it!"

As soon as the boars devoured pieces of the spirit fruit, they were a glow in a bright blue aura. Their angry eyes dilated and their angry grunts and growls became sweet piggy oinks. When they finished, the beasts simply squeaked gently and walked towards the exit of the village.

"You're welcome!" Jaz said, waving his hand. "Nothing bolder than dressing like a prissy princess. Even as a damsel, I'm cooler than tied up Taylor!" He stuck out his tongue. "No way was I gonna let my sister flirt with those guys."

Flora grinned from ear to ear. She had certainly accomplished her final task on this planetoid before they flew off to save it. And she couldn't wait to tell her bestie soulmate all about it.

Flora grinned. "Now that's what I call a Boar Appetit!"

Aya walked in the direction of the coast with Jeeg and Flora, her body wrapped tightly in fresh clothes Mrs. Du Bois had given her.

Flora was still full of adrenaline and her thin body jittered a little as Aya expressed her gratitude to her. "Flora, in all these years I've known you. I could never imagine you doing something so daring. I know, I know we've been over this, but I'm not over it! You're my hero!"

Flora's words buzzed with excitement too. "You always put your life on the line for me. If I don't step up, then I don't deserve you." She blushes a deep red. "Besides, I'd never let that rake mess with you."

Aya rubbed her hands together with a slapping motion. "Thanks for helping me take out the trash. You're the best friend I could ever ask for."

Flora grinned so hard it almost looked like a cringe to Aya. She was silent, so Aya went on. "Let's get me some clothes and head to the meeting. I need to hear what the town's plan is so I know how to help them."

REGRET & RECONCILIATION

Chapter 12

They went along the sandy path to Jeeg and Aya's shining cabin; but as they reached the tiny front porch, they saw Old Wing sitting in front of it.

Jeeg walked over to Old Wing with a smile.

Aya felt surprise when he walked up and pet the old Wyrmwolf without as much as a nip at his hand. "Why if it isn't Old Wing."

"You know him?" Aya's voice raised.

Jeeg gave a caring old laugh as he reflected on times past. "Why I cared for him after he had a dire fight. I had to amputate his wing because it had grown diseased and sickly. This was a long while ago."

Aya was happy that one of her friends already had repartee with Old Wing, but Flora was quite the opposite. The adrenaline buzz Flora was feeling wore off and with an "eek" she jumped behind Aya.

"Best friends in Wyrmwolf form are one thing. But I'll let you and Jeeg handle the real ones."

"No need to fear," Aya said, turning to her best friend. "He is a friend, but first, I need to speak with my associate."

Aya looked down at her tattoo to see the visage of Eterna growling and foaming at the mouth. "He is no friend of mine," said Eterna. "I'd rather make amends with the Thunderboar clan."

Aya's eyes grew compassionate for the scorn of her spirit guide, having been scorned herself. She took another look at Old Wing. He

145

looked miserable in broad daylight. Any hint of his cocky demeanor had long since seeped from his expression. She felt compassion for both of them and decided it would be best to play the peacemaker. "Eterna?"

"Yes child?"

"Would you believe that when I spoke to him in Wyrmwolf form, he told me he wanted to apologize to you?"

Eterna turned her head to look at him before snarling. "Tell him that I'd tear his apology limb from limb."

Aya's ears twitched and she held Eterna closer to her. "That's not all he said. He told me that he'd rather be known as the mate of the great Eterna, than the leader of the pack."

For the first time, Eterna's eye shone and the tone of her voice changed. "Surely you're putting me on."

"He learned his lesson when he lost all of his respect as an alpha male. He spent the time after your fight as a one-winged outcast that hid in the shadows."

Eterna's desires for blood seemed to retract in favor of a womanly reflection of empathy. Her fight with a Noctursa had left her crippled in a similar manner. The next time she opened her mouth, her tone had altered to exclude gruffness. "Does he really wish to apologize to me?"

Aya walked over to Old Wing who was still being doted on by Jeeg.

Eterna began to flinch in fear. "No I don't want him to see me like this. I uh…"

Aya held out her arm in front of Old Wing to show his cringing ex-lover with a panicked look on her face. Of course, only Aya could see her feelings of bashfulness and embarrassment. To Old Wing, she was just a stationary tattoo inked into Aya's skin.

When he saw Eterna on her skin, however, his head sank down. He lowered it in a bow and let out a soft and gentle whine.

Eterna stopped panicking and settled down herself listening to his soft puppyish whine. "He says to me: I didn't know what you meant to me until I felt your claws tear at my flesh. You may as well have torn out my heart. I'm deeply sorry."

Eterna's face retracted in shock, but slowly, her eye returned to her former lover. "Tell him... I didn't want the rest of his life to be like that for him. I hated him but never completely."

Aya relayed her message to Old Wing's ragged ears before Eterna spoke again. "And tell him, I begrudgingly accept his apology."

"She accepts your apology, Old Wing." Aya said, as the sorry animal continued to bow.

His face eased gently; and Jeeg, no stranger to a tormented romantic relationship spoke himself. "Old Wing. I know your forest has grown to become a dangerous place. Would you mind rooming with an old codger, his young friend, and your young pup?"

Old Wing looked up with a start, recognizing that his young pup Gardenia was in the house. He looked to Eterna again. Who whispered to Aya.

"She says 'Please, look after her,'" Aya repeated to Old Wing. "'She's the future of the forest.'"

Old Wing raised his body with newfound pride and purpose.

Aya felt overjoyed to have reunited Eterna's family, but she had things more important that celebrating to attend to. She looked to Jeeg who had risen with the old Wyrmwolf. "What did I miss at the meeting?"

"Nothing much, Aya. It was mostly Du Bois telling us that even though he values opinions, it's he who will make the final decision."

Aya rolled her eyes. "Sounds like standard Du Bois."

The Du Bois family laid claim to what they deemed an uncivilized planetoid hundreds of years ago, and everyone treated each chosen male successor of the first Colonel Du Bois with the same respect they gave him.

Aya did not like how very few ever went against what he said; but in the case of what Jeeg said next about Du Bois' plan, she felt that she would have to.

"Oh," said Jeeg raising his finger, "he had raised a preposition that we should hunt the animals now that fruit doesn't grow anymore."

Aya scowled and shook her head. Her young face wrinkled like Jeeg's comment had aged her twenty years. "Come on, we need to get going before he makes any more cockamamie decisions that doom this planet further."

Jeeg and Flora, both dressed in draping clothes ran with Aya, picking up their tailing fabric as they ran. He hollered to Aya as she ran with target-like precision towards the beer barn. "I was going to tell him exactly what happened on Tarabos, but Flora came in telling us about you and Old Wing."

Aya turned her head to Jeeg and nodded as they dashed through the center of town. "Don't worry, Jeeg. I know you weren't being lazy this time. Let's hurry though."

Reaching the beer barn, Aya dashed up the steps to the second story. Her bare feet running along the cracked, old and unrefined spirit wood. It bent with each determined step; and when she cracked the door wide open, it practically swung off its hinges. Everyone from young to old stared at Aya, curious why she was entering the building in such a dramatic fashion.

Aya knew that each of them had a differing opinion on her, ranging from seeing her as an utter nuisance to a charming oddity, but she hoped they'd all listen. They all had looks of concern on their faces.

Aya could feel their desperation as she stood there before speaking loud and clear. "Du Bois," she cried out, "I have been to the Nature's Gate and I have something to relay to you."

Du Bois, standing at the center of the people, raised his ginger eyebrow. "Earian spawn, when I said you could join us," he leveled his hand to aim right for her head, "I didn't mean for you to burst in like you do with everything else. This is a grave matter and I will not have your biased tree-hugging ways interfere with the future of my village."

Aya's face reddened with the first word of his sentence. She could shrug it off when everyone else said it. After all, they were ignorant about how much it hurt her; but for Du Bois, he knew it boiled her blood. It was a word he used to signal her as the outsider whose ways would be alien no matter how much she struggled to benefit the village. If there wasn't a sea of people blocking them from each other, Aya would have gone right at him, but instead her voice raged and a sharp vein burst from her neck. "Du Bois, it's you who's interfering with the future of everyone. We don't have the luxury of dealing with your ego right now."

Jeeg and Flora quickly squeezed in from the door past Aya, despite her feet being firmly planted on the ground. He raised his robed hand and placed it on Aya's shoulder. She brushed it aside while keeping her tunnel vision directly at Du Bois, but Jeeg spoke anyway. "Aya, you have to respect Mr. Du Bois. He is the leader of these people and they have chosen him to guide them."

This got Aya's attention and she gave another burst of emotion toward Jeeg. "But he doesn't understand anything and he doesn't want to."

"Aya, remember what I told you about presuming for everyone," Jeeg said, urgently trying to not get Aya ejected from this meeting. "Sit and listen to everyone's viewpoint, then speak your own."

Mr. Du Bois smile stretched from under his mustache. "Jeeg, your earian race yields smart elders," he said, ushering for them to sit down. "I hope one day, your spawn will grow to be as sensitive as you about dire matters."

Jeeg humbly bowed. His humility or in Aya's opinion, butt kissing, allowed them a place in the meeting.

"Besides," Du Bois said, "I always like to hear from everyone after I'm done talking. Maybe if such an impetuous child can hold her tongue, I will listen to what she has to say."

150

Aya glared at him; but then looked to Jeeg, and realized the wisdom in his words. She'd have her chance at Mr. Du Bois, but she'd have to wait it out. She glanced down at Eterna and the elder Wyrmwolf's face silently read the same thing. They pushed their way through the crowd.

Aya saw someone sitting behind Du Bois in a bar chair. It was Taylor. He was tied very tightly to the chair with both his arms and his legs banded in the same knots used to keep Noctursas out of a sack of fruits. Even with arms bound so tight and his blood seemingly drained from his arms, he still maintained a relaxed expression. It was almost admirable how he could behave like a complete scoundrel in front of the whole town, destroying their very way of sanctity and still retaining that same calm, self-satisfied look on his face. It was in stark contrast to the angry, red, hateful face of Mr. Du Bois.

Aya stood still, tapped her foot and generally looked displeased to see those two still in such close proximity.

Du Bois paced back and forth with an angry grimace on his face. "As I was saying before I was rudely interrupted. Up until fifteen years ago, we had always hunted animals. Not for sport as these earians will lead you to believe, but out of necessity."

There was muttering in the crowd from some of the older adults who had been around for this. Aya could hear them reminiscing about when they hunted, and how it was so much easier than when they had to wait for Aquans to soothe the beasts.

Aya had to bite her tongue because she could not stand how much these humans wanted to take the easy way out. But only out of respect for Jeeg, she remained silent.

Du Bois cordially extended his right hand to Jeeg. "When you convinced my father, rest his soul to partake in your rituals, our planetoid was peaceful. Now fruit is truly hard to obtain and mad beasts are roaming the planetoid."

Du Bois held his heart and with a breath outward, "I think it's time we returned to the ways before you came. What do you say Jeeg?"

Jeeg's brow wrinkled further than it was. It often shifted when he was deep in thought, and this discussion put him more on the spot than he'd ever like to be.

Aya knew he cared about the planetoid, but this did nothing to help her frustration. She couldn't talk, but he could. "Even in a situation as grave as this one, it is unwise to kill off the beasts of this planet."

"Why do you say that?" asked Du Bois.

Jeeg's brow wrinkled further. If it were a shirt, it would never be able to be pressed with a hot iron. He gritted his remaining teeth. "Du Bois, I never told you the conditions of our planet when we came here that fateful day."

"Well, speak of them now then," the town's colonel ordered.

Jeeg's eyes cast back to a date, a date he hoped would be fully eroded from his memory with his old age. "One day, about sixteen years ago, a leviathan attacked my village. It loomed near, bringing ice and snow, killing much of our tropical produce. When it reared its head, I could see it bore elder markings."

Aya barely remembered this day herself. She was a small child who was ordered by her parents to stay inside her cot until the danger had passed. This was the first time she heard about the beast's elder markings, something her good friend Eterna bore as well. The power of ice and snow was something Eterna yielded when she attacked Aya so the Aquan made a mental note of the similarities between her and the leviathan.

All the while Taylor gazed at her from behind Du Bois with the same partially relaxed, partially teasing eyes and smile. She responded with the look a savage beast gives another that has threatened its well-being.

"It killed many members of our village," Jeeg croaked with sudden sorrow. "It took many important people from me...from us. So, as the village elder, I...killed it."

Everyone looked at Jeeg as he choked out those words. They were puzzled that such a docile old man was capable of taking down a mighty dragon, a dragon that belonged only to the myths and legends that Jeeg spoke of when he relayed stories to the village children. Her mentor, still overcome by emotion and trauma from the event, gazed at the ground as he leaned on his staff. "I should have soothed it like we did the beasts here. I was fully capable of it, but I let my rage overpower my better judgement."

"I'm sorry to hear that," Du Bois said, even he showed sympathy in his eyes. "What was the result?"

"It deeply disturbed the planet's core," said Jeeg, attempting to regain his wits. "The planet had lost one of its guardians; and one day, as you all know, our planet imploded."

Everyone gasped and looked at Jeeg with abject horror. Aya began to feel like she didn't need to convince anyone at all. She was disappointed since she desperately wanted to lash Du Bois with her own words, but quickly realized that she was being petty like he was.

Du Bois seemed moved by Jeeg, and all that remained was the matter of getting everyone off the planet like Nature's Gate had asked.

Taylor continued to taunt her with his facial expression; but when she met his gaze this time, she realized she had a plan. People began to hound Du Bois over his hasty decision to hunt again and even his tall and imposing presence didn't faze a group of terrified and angry people.

Aya quickly whispered to Jeeg, and he raised his hand, much to Du Bois' relief.

"Quiet everyone! Hey! Jeeg is going to speak again!" Du Bois shouted at the top of his lungs. "If you want to know how the devil we're going to get out of this life-or-death situation, you better listen to him."

Slowly the crowd quieted.

Jeeg stepped forward. "Well, it's not me who has an idea, it's Aya."

He stepped to the side and let Aya walk forward.

Everyone began to quietly rabble again. It wasn't that they didn't trust Aya, but they believed that the best plan of action could only come from an Aquan far beyond her years.

"Jeeg, you're really going to let this earian spawn hold the floor?" asked Du Bois, accosting Jeeg. "She better have a damn good plan."

Flora dashed to the center and yelled out loud in her now-shrill voice. "Please everyone, give her a chance. I have full faith in Aya. She wants the best for us and our planetoid."

Aya exchanged glances with her friend, both had a smile on their face as they looked into each other's eyes. "Thanks Flor," she said with her eyes beaming as bright as her smile.

Taylor's loud voice mocked them, "Why don't you two get a room. Nothing you say will help these people."

"Funny you say that," Aya shouted back, "because we're going to need your help to save the planetoid."

Everyone's voices raised in shock. How was this knavish man going to help them? It was he who had put them in this predicament even if they didn't know that. All they knew was he was a trouble maker who tried to use his newfound status to have an innocent person killed.

Aya crossed her arms. "Mr. Spaceman came here on his spaceship, didn't he? The very same ship that…"

She paused. She wanted to tell everyone of Taylor's mistake that caused this apocalyptic scenario, but she feared that this knowledge would only fill the people with hate. A part of her wanted to see him pay for his crime, but right now she needed him.

"Of course," Taylor stuttered, fear twinkling in his eyes. "It's a very sturdy vessel. A humble and grateful ship."

"Well," Aya said, still feeling triumphant while ignoring him. "Can't one of us use the spaceship to fly to another planetoid and get help? Maybe we can convince Taylor's planet to lend us some spaceships to evacuate everyone from this planetoid. Just so you know, I spoke with Nature's Gate and we agreed an evacuation of the whole planetoid was the best plan."

Aya could see with how everyone talked amicably among themselves that they were considering her plan. It only took a highly skeptical Gully to burst her bubble. "Does anyone actually know how to pilot his spaceship? Or any spaceship for that matter?"

There was a resounding hail of 'no' in response before they fell silent. All of a sudden, someone in the back hollered, "why don't you do it Aya?"

"You're our protector, Aya! You should help us!" Allons hollered.

One mother cried, "think of our children, Aya. This has to work."

"I don't want to leave my home," an old man shouted. "I've lived here all my life. It's the only home I've known."

People began to agree and disagree left and right, and Aya trembled in response. She didn't fear man, nor beast, nor bird, but the one thing that unnerved her more than anything was flight. She looked around nervously, feeling overwhelmed by those cheering her and demanding she be their hero. She gazed down at Eterna who seemed to understand immediately that she needed some guidance. "You rode me just fine child, and you were in a violent storm. I know you could pilot this rake's ship if you went purely by instinct."

Aya nodded her head nervously before finding her arm grabbed by Flora. "Don't worry, love," she raised Aya's hand "I'm going to pilot this ship for Aya."

"You're doing what?!" Aya turned purely out of curiosity to see Mr. and Mrs. Du Bois' with both of their mouth's hung open.

Jaz cheered and raised his arms excitedly. "Yeah, you go big sister!"

Aya could see Flora smile broadly, feeling more energized by Jaz's response than her parents. He never looked up to Flora, thinking she was incredibly prissy and girly. This was the first time Jaz ever cheered Flora for anything.

Flora spoke boldly to her parents. "I'm going to do this. I feel useless on this planetoid and I'll change what y'all think of me. I want to go to other worlds. I want to help this one too like Aya always has."

Mr. Du Bois was clearly flustered, but he wanted to remain firm over the control of his daughter. "What if I say I won't let you, Flora?"

Flora placed her hands on her hips and walked right up to her father. There was a clear height difference, but Flora made sure to make her words defiant and imposing. "Then I'll never forgive you. You view me as nothing but a delicate porcelain doll; but because of Aya, I've grown. I stood up to a full-grown Wyrmwolf. I'm not about to submit to you," she said, her body shaking. "And I...I've always wanted to leave this place. I know I can be so much more beyond this planetoid."

Aya wanted to applaud her friend. She had known about Flora's ambitions for years, but this was the first time she voiced them in front of her father; and not only him, in front of the entire village no less. "All in favor of letting us try to fly that ship?"

There was a resounding cry of affirmation from half the room. Aya, Jaz and the rest of the Du Bois children joined in as the parents just stood in silence. Some of the older folks still protested about leaving the planetoid, their old conservative ways firmly rooting them to this planet's soil.

Du Bois raised his non-bandaged hand. "Silence!"

Everyone looked at Du Bois with eager eyes waiting for his response. "I will decide tonight. This is clearly an emergency and we need help as soon as possible. Flora, Aya and Jeeg, I want you to at least inspect the scoundrel's ship. Everyone else can retire. Meeting adjourned."

Aya's heart pounded heavily, but not as heavily as Flora's.

"That was so scary!" Flora said, red and shaking.

Aya patted her friend's head. "And you faced that fear with bravery and elegance."

Flora buried her blush against Aya's shoulder.

As everyone exited the beer barn, the two walked alongside each other in silence. They both were mentally preparing for an adventure. Though Du Bois hadn't consented to anything yet, he was clearly left with no other choice.

Both women had their motivations: Aya wished to be a guardian of this planetoid and Flora dreamed of being self-sufficient. Both hoped this was a brand-new road that led to their goals, but this road was long and uncertain. They each took respite in each other's company. It gave them confidence and a good friend to fall back on.

THE STARSHIP

Chapter 13

Aya and Flora asked around where Taylor left his spaceship and it was only young Jaz who seemed to know. He was leaving the beer barn with his numerous siblings and mother who strained to keep watch over them all.

"After we explored Jaz Island," Jaz chimed in, quite proud he knew something the village didn't, "he used some kind of wee-mote can-troll thingy and parked the ship on Jaz Island.

"Thanks Jaz," Flora said, smiling warmly.

"Are you really going to fly the ship like you said?" Jaz asked.

Flora boldly laid her hands on her hips and gave her best interpretation of Aya. "I didn't say it for nothing."

All of Flora and Jaz's brothers and sisters chimed in with the kind of childish admiration of their eldest sister.

"Flora, you're so cool," one said.

"I want I want to be just like you, big sis," another said.

Flora's pale complexion was prone to redness, but she rarely blushed as red as that moment. "Well, I do say..." she remarked in her sweet country accent.

Aya patted her friend on the back. "We should go before you get too starstruck." She seized her friend by her hand and led her away.

Flora's head was still swimming in the praise her younger family members had soaked her in. As they walked to the lakeside, Aya began to realize that Flora was more than a soft, fragile belle. Aya knew she would have to be brave to fly in Taylor's deathtrap. At the time, she was more curious about what her friend felt as they walked from the wooden village to the sandy pathways lined by yellow grass, hand in hand.

"Flor, I really like what's gotten into you," Aya said with an appreciative tone.

Flora returned her words with a shy look. "Well to tell you the truth, you have Aya. Seeing my friend in danger made me realize I can't stay meek." Flora's voice grew thin and emotional as she spoke. "I want to protect you too."

"I'm blessed to have you." Aya's eyes sparkled. "And I can assure you I'm not going anywhere. Trust me, with you, Eterna and Jeeg in my corner, I have one helluva team."

Aya received equally approving glances from both Flora and Eterna's inky visage on her arm.

Feeling nothing would come between them, they were ready for their next journey as well. They reached the lakeside where water lapped the sand. In the late afternoon they could see the glint of Taylor's ship perched on the third floating island to the left, a good distance from them, but not totally unreachable by bubble.

When Aya informed Flora of this, she grew a bit nervous. She had never traveled in one of her bubbles because her parents had deemed swimming in it "uncouth for a proper lady." Flora didn't like swimming in general.

Aya smirked a little when she saw Flora hesitating. "So you'll fly in Taylor's ship, but not my bubbles?"

"My lawrd, I just don't want to get my dress soaked," Flora chided back.

Aya crossed her arms and rolled her eyes in a friendly way. "You could always shed it. After all we have bigger problems right now."

"Y-y-y-ou're right. I mean, you went around naked, so I can…at least do this much. I do hope nobody sees me doing this," Flora shot back and lifted her sundress over her head, hastily undressing to her undergarments and removing her large sun hat in the process.

She stood there bashfully covering up her skinny body. Her knees were pasty and knobby and Aya always had a good laugh when she saw them. They looked like they belonged to some pale creature from the underground. She shivered a little too in the light afternoon breeze. "Aya, come on, I don't like standing out here like this."

"I forgot that some of us aren't used to wearing aerodynamic clothing," Aya teased. She then turned to the matter at hand, and began to conjure up a bubble with her staff along with the rhythmic movement of her fish tattoos. She looked out the side of her eyes and watched as Flora shivered, observing the water slowly circle until it formed up into a mass while biting her lip. "Your chariot awaits, princess." Aya stuck her tongue out and leapt into her bubble.

"I'm not a princess," says Flora, turning an even deeper shade of red.

"You're a tomato princess." Aya popped her head out. "This is another reason why I wear light clothing. It makes bubble travel less of a pain."

Aya could see her friend tremble a little so she reached out her hand and slowly Flora grasped it, before walking to her bubble.

161

Flora dipped her finger in and made a sour face. "It's so cold."

"Well, there's two ways of getting used to being in water. Slowly wading yourself in or…" Aya's face displayed an expression that normally belonged the wiliest of Aquans "you just dive right in." She yanked her friend forward, who let out an eek before getting fully submerged in Aya's bubble before they took off.

The two flew through the sky. Aya seeing that Flora was frantically covering her mouth, grabbed her friend and they swam up to the top of the bubble.

Flora let out a big gasp and shook her drenched ginger hair. "Why I never would do such a dirty, under-handed thing."

"Yeah, but I would," Aya said, sticking her tongue out. "We can't wait for you to be ready. Everyone is counting on us!"

Aya could see her friend was no longer paying attention, but was holding her hands up in the air as they soared.

"Whoa, golly. This is actually kind of fun!" Flora exclaimed. "I always had a feeling I'd like flying and this is the closest I've ever been to it."

Aya frowned and muttered under her breath. "This is as much flying as I'd really want to do. And you better get used to flying if you're going to pilot Taylor's junk ship."

Aya released Flora from her bubble and they both dropped onto the floating piece of stone with Taylor's ship neatly parked on it. It gleamed in the sunlight and the light shone in Flora's eyes.

"Whoa this thing is so cool," Flora said looking up at the vehicle. "I wonder if he left it open?"

Flora had forgotten how cold she was and began to tinker with the cockpit. "I've always dreamed about spaceships but it's been so long since I've actually seen one. The last time was when you crashed on our planetoid and…into my life."

It was Aya's turn to shiver, but she shook off the thought of the wreckage and loss. "Let's just find how to open this thing."

Flora's eyes darted to a small latch on the ship's underside. It was small, dark and grey. It contrasted with the ship's blue and purple coloring. She hooked her fingers into it, and marveled as the ship's underside opened like a door. She climbed into its interior and found a button on the ship's small control panel with a shape of the glass window on it.

Aya was completely bewildered when her friend disappeared, having been leaning on the cockpit in the hope that she could find an opening there. Without warning, (for Aya at least) the cockpit slid back and Aya fell into the ship's cockpit with a scream.

"Hey Aya, I found the way inside!" her friend exclaimed.

Aya quickly rose onto the cushioned seat, shaking her slightly frazzled head. "You don't say, Flor." She soon observed that the inside, though comfy with tan insolated seats, was a tad crammed. There was only a pilot seat and two passenger seats behind it. Aya's feet ached at thinking of being confined in it for weeks on end. She leaned up on the seat and watched her friend tinker with the control panel. Something caught her attention that was completely unrelated to the panel itself. It was a crude bobble toy of a nude woman placed on the dashboard. Its butt jiggled as Aya leaned forward on the ship.

"What is this man's fixation with butt spasms?" Aya looked to Flora with questions in her eyes.

"He doesn't care about that, Aya." Flora groaned in return.

Aya's eyes and curiosity were quickly drawn to something underneath it. "Flor, look under the figure."

Flora quickly grabbed it and held it up. It was a photograph of a person who seemed out-of-this-world to both Aya and Flora. The visage was a woman of undetermined years. Her hair was as bright white-yellow as white lightning. Though her face was completely smooth, she had an adult air to her that made her look like she could have been anywhere from thirty-five to fifty-five. She wore thick rimmed glasses, a low-cut pants suit and had a powerful commanding grip on a customized thunderbolt shaped pen; all signifying she was a strong-willed business woman with a sense of calculation like a buzzwasp. Her hair was tied back in a long, electrifying ponytail, spilling out in a jagged way, and underneath her eyes were thick zigzag patterns drawn on by eyeliner. It was clear to Aya that electricity and its deadly nature were a central motif for this woman.

Upon closer inspection from both Flora and Aya, they shared their divisive opinions on the photograph. "There's something fake about that woman," Aya decreed with narrowed eyes.

"I dunno, Aya. She's very stylish for a woman of her age. I like her interesting sense of fashion," her friend responded.

"You like any girl who is fashionable." Aya laughed and pointed a thumb towards herself.

"True. Hey what's this written on the back?"

Flora turned the photo around to show Aya what she had caught a glimpse of. Written on the back in fancy penmanship was a little message: "Taylor, you got the world in the palm of your hand, baby."

Aya pondered upon who this woman was. What was her significance to Taylor? Was she his mom? His lover? Aya had a feeling she wouldn't know until she talked to the king of sleaze himself.

They felt a jerk of the ship, Flora screamed and dropped the picture to hold onto the control panel.

Aya grasped onto the seat. "Flor! What are you doing?" she asked, closing her eyes as she shook.

"I don't know. I swear I didn't touch the control panel until the ship stirred."

The ship slowly began to rise causing Aya to scream in a voice much more girlish than her deep assured tone. "Please Flor, just land this thing."

Flora began to hastily push buttons as the ship began to soar, but a female voice resonated from the control panel. "Control panel lockdown. Sit back and enjoy the flight."

Aya cried as she covered her eyes, wishing she was anywhere else, but Flora kept her eyes open and remained energized. She was enjoying the flight and with a free "oh yeah!" she threw her arms in the air and let go of the essence of being a proper lady that her parents had painstakingly enforced upon in her. She felt truly free for the first time since she was born and her attire and screaming voice reflected it. She didn't even care where the ship was taking her, she just enjoyed the flight.

The ship took them to the coast where a small group of people were stationed. The ship landed with a "now entering landing mode" and soon rested on the ground.

Flora noticed the people standing before her. Jeeg, her mother and father, Taylor and two of the larger farmers stood to greet them and one of the farmers had a rapier fixed at Taylor's throat.

Taylor hastily manipulated a small black device in his hand, which was presumably the ship's remote.

Flora was so full of excitement she didn't realize she was standing dripping wet in her undergarments with her hands raised high, showing off her neatly shaven under arms to the world.

"Flora, why in san hill are you standing in your skivvies in a spaceship?" Mr. Du Bois said, his face an angry shade of red. "Come down this instant."

Flora's shame and meekness returned instantly to her and she wrapped her arms around her body. "Oh dear, I'm so sorry."

"Is that earian girl up there? Did she convince you to behave like a shameless wild animal, like her?"

Upon closer inspection they soon saw that Aya was too busy rolling on the floor of the ship to even combat Du Bois' use of derogatory names. She had not been on a spaceship since the day she fled her collapsing planet and crashed on this planetoid. She feared the ship

166

would lose control like hers had. She hoped with all her heart that Flora would be able to tame this wild vehicle.

Both women stepped down, and Flora reinserted herself into her dress, the people standing around them were filled with curiosity.

"Daddy," Flora asked at last, "have you finally decided to give us your blessing…on this journey." She fiddled with her hair.

Du Bois looked hesitant and brushed his mustache. It was only when his wife gave him a mighty glare that he finally spoke. "I was going to say no, but then somebody got to me."

Flora's mother stepped forward. She had a lively youthfulness in her eyes, something that often wasn't present in the mothers in the village. "Dear, you won me over completely when I heard you stand up to your father." She put her frail white arms around Mr. Du Bois and held him close to her shoulder. "I love my husband deeply, but a moment hasn't gone by where I think I settled down too soon."

Aya could see Flora tremble with emotion when she realized Mrs. Du Bois finally understood her.

"Saving our people is the most important thing," her mother continued, "I do hope you have a grand adventure on the way."

"Oh mom," Flora cried and hugged her.

"I'm letting you go, daughter," Du Bois said, sternly. "And I will convince the people that this is the best plan of action. But you better remember us and represent the Du Bois family crest in the best way possible."

"I will, daddy. Thank you," Flora said softly, looking up at him.

The burly mustached man, hardly a sentimentalist got behind his wife and daughter and embraced them. "I'm going to miss complaining about you. What am I gonna chat about at the bar now?" he asked, combing her hair and smiling.

Aya smiled at the family's warm embrace, but then she noticed Taylor glaring at her with a smirk on his face. "Why is he here?" she demanded to Mr. Du Bois with an angry glare to match.

"This ruffian had two choices, either he was going to rot with the rest of us, or he's going to help you with your mission." Du Bois whacked Taylor's head hard, temporarily knocking the smirk off his face to Aya's delight. "See he's part of a company that owns a lot of spaceships and he's going to convince them to save us with his silver tongue. Unless that was a lie too."

Aya crossed her arms, frowning in displeasure. "He better not backstab us."

Taylor shot back with a candid look. "Honestly, I just want to get out of this hell myself. But there's something I want to ask you alone, Aquan."

Aya sensed the ensuing conversation had something to do with his past behavior. Perhaps he'd feign regret and would inauthentically grovel to her about what he did and the trouble it landed him. That at least sounded entertaining to her.

"Okay," she said, "but I'm not going near him unarmed."

Du Bois nodded, and the burly bearded farmer holding Taylor's neck hostage handed the rapier to Aya. The other farmer removed the remote from Taylor's hand and bound his hands back together.

Aya positioned the sword at Taylor's neck with an even greater intensity than the farmer did, causing Taylor to draw tense gasps. When they were far away enough from everyone else, Taylor spoke. "Being so close to you, I can feel the way you breathe. So hostile and agitated. I must have hit a nerve"

"You can drop the power play, Taylor. I'm fully in control here," Aya said, angling the sword with even more of a slant.

"That you are, that you are," Taylor scoffed as his voice deepened. "And because you are, I want you to tell me something."

"What?"

"Why haven't you told them what I did? Surely, you've had the chance to by now."

Aya paused for a second before realizing Taylor was still trying desperately to get the upper hand. "Let's just say, the people of this planetoid aren't as forgiving as I am."

"How so?"

"They hadn't done it in a long time," Aya's face stretched to form a dark smile, "but they would have sent you to the gallows."

Taylor's sharp sneer teetered a bit, and she could see him grit his teeth more. He fully believed her. "Any reason why you would save me after what I did to you?"

"I'll never forget you." Aya smirked. "But let's just say I didn't want to add more drama to the situation."

Taylor laughed a cold dry laugh. "Aquan women, as cryptic as always."

Aya and Taylor walked back in their uncomfortable position when Aya handed the sword off to the farmer again. More people had arrived, this time bearing fruits. Some also had rummaged through the ship and found some space suits. They were waiting to pack everything inside, but first, the newly christened female astronauts had to prepare themselves.

Jeeg greeted Aya with a warm hug. "Well, it seems like you'll be going soon." The elder's voice shook.

"Really?" Aya exclaimed. "But Flora doesn't know how to fly yet."

"There's something called auto pilot, Du Bois says, I don't know what kind of magic it is, but it will do the work for you." Jeeg added a little aside under his breath. "I wish I could put my chores on auto pilot."

Aya put her tight hand on Jeeg's shoulder and gave him a firm embrace. "You know, you can't slack off just yet, old man. The whole planetoid's depending on you too."

"I'm well aware," the old man said with resignation. "We must prepare you to leave. I'm going to miss you so much. To think, this is the first time we've been apart for nearly fifteen years."

Aya felt like crying, but she held it back. "I wouldn't have it any other way, my old friend."

Jeeg's bushy eyebrows softened against his old wrinkled skin and Aya could tell that was the response he longed to hear. "Good. Is there anything else I need to know?"

"Yes," Aya said, "the Nature's Gate requires you to visit it and perform a ritual of some sort. I don't know what."

"Ah the restoration ritual," Jeeg replied. "That's going to give these old bones a work out."

"You know of it?"

Yes," Jeeg said sadly, and he looked down. "It was what our planet required, but I failed to provide." HIs head rose and he stood as straight as his arched back would allow. "I will not let these people down."

"I know you won't," Aya said, embracing him once more.

Eterna barked and Aya looked at her. "Tell him it means so much to me that he's taking care of my family."

Aya relayed Eterna's message and Jeeg responded. "Don't worry, Old Wing and I will be like a pair of moms."

Aya gave a hearty laugh and her tattoo smiled. She bowed to Jeeg and walked to the crowd.

Flora had already dressed herself in a space suit. It was made of a very thick cream-colored baggy material complete with a helmet that slid up. He looked a little consumed by it, but she still stood with total confidence in herself and her mission.

"Aya hurry up," she cried, "we can't be late to save the planetoid."

Aya ran to them. Taylor had already been restrained in a space suit of his own and had seated himself in the third seat of the spaceship.

"Ready when you are captain," he said, trying to bring levity to people's fixed glares at him.

Aya fit herself into her own baggy space suit. It was so restricting. There was no way she could dash through the forest with this tied to her body. Space travel must have required one to be very dense and restricted.

Aya climbed up on the ship's wing before fitting into the close space that was her seat in the cockpit. Pulling the diagonal straps across her chest, she felt as packed in like the other cargo.

Flora had climbed her way in too. She began to tinker with the controls in the front seat. "Which one is the auto-pilot?"

"The auto pilot only activates on my voice command," Taylor said with a boast from his precarious position.

"Standing by at your service, Mr. Lunsford." The auto pilot's soft female voice said as if to mock Flora.

Flora pulled out the remote-control tablet. She began to press it haphazardly until a wave of text appeared on its screen. "To reset designated captain command system, hold down all four corners of the control pad screen," she read aloud. "Aha!"

Flora spread two fingers on each hand across the corners of the pad screen and as the auto pilot repeated its "Standing by at your service Mr. Lunsford," its feminine voice grew deep and robotic until it ceased. "Auto pilot reset. Insert name of new captain."

"Flora Du Bois."

The voice changed back to its friendly, feminine tone. "Welcome to your first voyage, Captain Du Bois."

"Captain Du Bois?" Flora fluttered her eyelashes and pointed to herself. "Me? Why I never."

"Better watch out," Aya said to Taylor as he shook his head "Flora gets on a bit of an ego trip when she's in charge. Fortunately, I have nothing to worry about."

172

Taylor in return just muttered to himself. "So fickle. And after all these years of treating her like a lady too."

"When will you realize it's just a machine?" Aya asked, trying to laugh amidst her own panic.

"Captain Du Bois, enter the coordinates for your next destination," the voice instructed Flora.

Flora gazed around nervously, realizing she hadn't a clue.

"The City Electric of the planet Aleatore," Taylor whispered.

"Ah yes, The City Electric, thanks swabbie," Flora responded.

"Coordinates now added, prepare for take-off," said the ship as the cockpit's glass window slid firmly over the three seats.

Aya watched with baited breath as her friends cleared for lift off. The ship slowly began to angle itself with the sky and with the help of some reusable rocket thrusters on the sides of its wings blasted itself into the sky with a loud crackle boom of electricity. Aya frantically gasped the seatbelt straps that held her in place as the ground and people grew more miniature and diorama like.

"I'm doing this. I'm doing this," Aya said, her tone warbling, terrified and not able to convince anyone including herself. Her chest rose and fell rapidly as her lungs danced in terror inside of her. She stifled a look to the window and saw just as the sky merged with stars.

Aya was off to see a whole new planetoid like she had done as a child; but this time, she hoped to bring with her not only her own life, but the lives of everyone else too. Everyone and the planetoid itself were all counting on her and she could not let them down.

She frowned but was put at ease when she saw her friend. It filled her heart with joy to see a human just as devoted to the planetoid as her. She knew this was the adventure she had always longed to go on. A journey to a whole new planetoid. She could not even imagine what she'd see, but she knew that every inch of this cosmic distance was part of the big dream, and she wanted to see every fragment of it.

STAY TUNED FOR FUTURE VOLUMES OF PLANETOID COMING 2025

Books from *Sphere of Compassion*

DANCE MAGIC

When free-spirited dancer Stella Grace arrives at the city of her dreams, she finds herself in a nightmarish world. In this techno metropolis where people harness the power of the elements through the motion of dance, rumors spread of party-goers being drained of their energy. Alongside her timid best friend Helen Wheels and fearful rival Dan Dorphin, Stella must uncover conspiracies and inner truths to liberate the corrupted city.

A magical techno-future adventure that explores the world of music and dance with whimsical style.

A Subversive PUNCH to the Face!

Join Main Character and Best Friend, two proud American otakus and ViralTube legends, who are pulled into another world and bribed into joining a growing conflict between victimized villages and deranged dictators. Anime tropes only lead to shattered expectations for our ego-driven hero! He is accompanied by awesome allies, protected by canonical plot armor, and armed with the power of Friendship (a vulgar rocket launcher who uses emotions as ammo). But will these and his encyclopedic knowledge of anime be enough to overcome the threats of a dimension hopping assassin, a guardian angel's sexual advances, a musclebound Amazonian, memory erasing mushrooms, a Fearsome Dragon, a charismatic king with a psychotic obsession for our hero and his army of cut throat cat boys? The Main Character is a 4th wall breaking parody packed with anime references, subversive characters and intense battles!

177

Be your own Hero!

Before she found the Hero of Destiny, Annie had her own journey!

Join Annie on her adventure through the epic dark fantasy world of The Main Character series! This young, loving and determined girl will team up with cursed heroes, adorable angels and mythical creatures to reunite with her cherished family! Will her bonds with her allies be enough to protect her from mechanized samurai, shadow hounds, rogue dimensional assassins and an army of CatBoy soldiers? Or will life's story be closed before she can write her happily ever after?

*This book can be read before OR after any book from **The Main Character** series.*

In a School of Assassins, Suffering is Growth.

Before Assailant encountered the Hero of Destiny, he crafted his own legend! Discover the dark origins of the fabled Broad-Spectrum assassin. Follow him through deadly exams, covert conspiracies and murderous missions all the while delving deep into the lore of the epic dark fantasy world of The Main Character series! This child of misfortune will work alongside cuddly killers, polymorphous monsters, enslaved heroes, and tragic angels to unravel the secrets hidden by the Assassin's Guild. Armed with mythic knowledge and guided by love, can he wield his truth to conquer skillful students, treacherous assassins, shadowy shapeshifters and secret organizations? Will his legends become a beacon of hope or a seed of despair?

*This book can be read before OR after any book from **The Main Character** series.*

In a world of monster clans and political mayhem, one angel seeks unity. Embark
on a fantastical journey with Amorita, a racoon angel on a mission to round up
monster girls all across the realm. These pairs of princesses and advisors are being
corralled for a competition that will turn these troubled princesses into fearless
queens. Riding upon a mobile motel for monsters, this angel will journey all across
the Kingdom to recruit these royal runaways. On her travels, she must overcome a
cursed forest run by territorial fairies, conquer a gem filled cave guarded by a dragon
and survive the wrath of a furry mafia boss' monster girl haven. Can this angel
manage to protect the monster girls under her watch and how long can she bear
watching their romantic missteps before breaking her vow of non-intervention?

Welcome to a new perspective on the ancient world of the The Main Character
series, that focuses on the local monsters instead of the foreign heroes.

*This book can be read before OR after any book from **The Main Character***
series.

Freedom is a Shackle.

Exp 8 is a living weapon. After awakening in an isolated lab, one instinct fuels him: a burning desire for freedom. His creator, Devlin, will stop at nothing to keep Exp 8 subservient to his will, even if it means sending droves of weaponized warriors to capture him. To break out of Devlin's hold, Exp 8 stages a rebellion, using both his wit and power to unite his fellow Exps against their creator. But not all enemies can be converted, and Devlin is not the only one with plans for the rogue weapon. The sentient inventions Exp 8 and his allies encounter become more powerful, fanatical and merciless with each wave. Driven by instinct and the desire to free his people, Exp 8 perseveres through conflict and loss. Is freedom worth the cost if he alone desires it?

A sci-fi anime-style experience packed with intense battles and other-worldly abilities.

181

Is clairvoyance a gift or a curse?
Before she became Fate, Ebui fought against her destiny.
Explore the ancient culture and traditions of the Ainu through the lens of a child. Ebui is a hopeful and brave girl who yearns to become a respected shaman of her village. Threats loom around every chapter of her life in the form of enemy tribes, violent ceremonies, sinister plots, and her own cursed prophecies. Will her hope survive through the supernatural storm of despair, or will her efforts bring about the end of her people?

Immerse yourself in the lives and backstories of characters from the *Of The Exps* series in the first of the Origins of the Exps novels!
This book can be read before any book from **Of The Exps** *series.*

On the Plus Side: Bubbly Tea (One-shot Comic)

SHOPPING SPREE

Stella is exhausted from her grueling training as a neon knight, the groovy protectors of the funky City Electric. To unwind, the rising starlet decides to take her teacher Jayden and her bestie Helen Wheels on a fun trip to the mall. Things don't turn out as expected and all the sudden they're thrown into a tricky situation that quickly escalates. Will the fizzy bubble tea after party brighten their moods or just cause more problems for the trio?

A bite-sized gateway drug into the magical techno-futuristic tale that explores the world of music and dance with whimsical style.

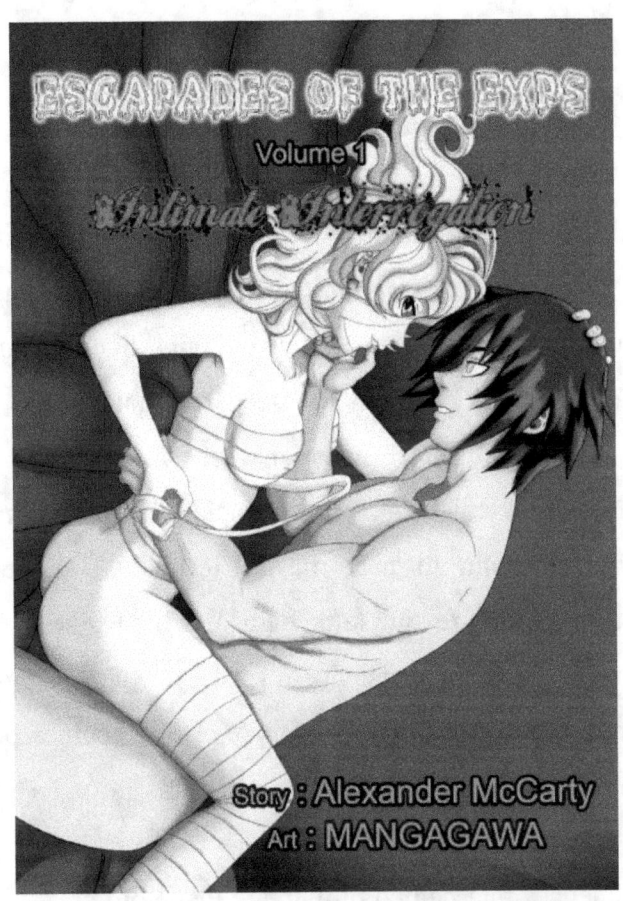

Is sex just another tool for an assassin?
The deadly girlfriend of Devlin's new crush is discovered in his bed. The seductive assassin has an offer for the hot-blooded scientist and will do whatever she must to seduce him to her cause.

Become entranced by the first Hentai Manga from *Of The Exps* series based on a scene from the ***Rebellion of the Exps: Exp 8*** novel.
*This manga can be read before any book from **Of The Exps** series.*

READ THE FULL COLOR NOW BY SIGNING UP

https://Patreon.com/Sphere_of_Compassion/

About the Author

Jhonny Steppes is a chronicler of secrets and a historian of the Aleatore planetoid. Once Daddy D took charge of the City Electric, Steppes dedicated himself to providing a bias free account of all the primary figures in this tumultuous period. Operating from an underground bunker, beneath the city, Stepps lives humbly on black beans and the affection from his Jeeg roommates. He is currently preparing for when the Edwardians resurface at the end of the millennium. His hobbies are scribing ancient text into a more modern language and listening to disco music. He feels art is the escape one needs to truly enjoy life and so he dedicates his life to it. He hopes to write something that connects with at least a few people and bring them further enjoyment and happiness in life. He welcomes people of all shapes and sizes to enjoy his art. By writing this story, he hopes to have accomplished this mission.

His influences that helped him create Planetoid are Avatar the Last Airbender, Princess Mononoke, Tolkien and the Tales of series.

Music that influenced him as well includes progressive rock bands Yes and Genesis. The song, White Mountain, by Genesis had a profound impact on the mood of this story.

Aya's Loving Request

Whether fur, feathered or scaled, all animals share a love of life. We are all creatures of the earth and should do our best to not intrude in the lives of others. I request you follow me on a natural lifestyle that neither partakes in the consumption of our animal neighbors nor the exploitation of their labor. On behalf of all the creatures of your world, I thank you for choosing to live Vegan!

If you need resources, the ones below are the absolute best.

http://www.adaptt.org/

http://www.abolitionistapproach.com/

veganeducationgroup.com

www.ingramcontent.com/pod-product-compliance
Lightning Source LLC
Chambersburg PA
CBHW061205170626
46809CB00003B/1246